DESTINED MATE

CATAMOUNT LION SHIFTERS, BOOK 4

J.H. CROIX

This is a work of fiction. Names, characters, businesses, places, events and incidents are either the products of the author's imagination or used in a fictitious manner. Any resemblance to actual persons, living or dead, or actual events is purely coincidental.

Copyright © 2016 J.H. Croix

All rights reserved.

Cover design by CT Cover Creations

No part of this book may be reproduced in any form or by any electronic or mechanical means, including information storage and retrieval systems, without written permission from the author, except for the use of brief quotations in a book review.

 Created with Vellum

DEDICATION

For the brilliant women who read romance!

***Sign up for my newsletter for information on
new releases!***
http://jhcroixauthor.com/subscribe/

Follow me!
jhcroix@jhcroix.com
https://amazon.com/author/jhcroix
https://www.bookbub.com/authors/j-h-croix
https://www.facebook.com/jhcroix
https://www.instagram.com/jhcroix/

ONCE UPON A TIME...

Centuries ago in the northern Appalachian Mountains, mountain lions fled deeper and deeper into the mountains, seeking safety from the rapid encroachment of humanity into their vast territory. Mountain lions developed the power to shift from human to mountain lion and back again, saving their species as they hid in plain sight. The majestic wild cats became creatures of myth. Reported sightings were treated as wildly speculative rumors. Impossible. Until one evening on a busy highway, a car struck an animal in the dark. The first confirmed sighting of a mountain lion in the East in close to seventy-five years. The wild cat was dead, its unbelievable existence snuffed out by a car. This mountain lion wasn't just any mountain lion. Though its autopsy would only reveal it was, in fact, a mountain lion and that the lion had improbably traveled over 1,500 miles from South Dakota, the longest known journey for such a creature. In Catamount, Maine, shifters lived amongst the world, having successfully protected their very existence for centuries. Until one of their own died an improbable death, and they learned of a threat facing their kind.

1
———

Shana Ashworth gritted her teeth as her feet slipped out from under her and she skidded onto the icy road. When her hip crashed against the pavement, she couldn't hold back her grunt. The pain seared through her. She unceremoniously came to a stop in the bramble of a bush beside the road. A bush that just happened to be wild rose with plenty of thorns on its bare branches. The early spring morning had tempted her for a run, and now she was paying a small price.

Her breath misted in the cool air. She remained where she was for the moment. The bare ground peeked out from the lingering snow cover. She leaned back on her hands, the icy pavement cold through her gloves. With a sigh, she glanced around. She was blessedly alone at the moment, although she was almost in the center of town. She tilted her face skyward and savored the warm sun. Buds were showing on the trees and birds were chattering like mad. Spring was technically here, but it would be another few weeks before the last of the snow as gone. Winter held onto Maine usually. Once it released its grip, the transition into spring was glorious in its contrast.

She gingerly shifted her weight and straightened her legs. Thorny branches clung to the fabric of her running tights. She tore them free and gathered her energy to stand. She was within a block of Roxanne's Country Store. Once she managed to get to her feet, she considered perhaps she should take a break at Roxanne's before trying to run home.

A short walk later, her hip protesting most of the way, Shana walked down the aisle toward the coffee shop in the back of the store. It was early yet, but the place was already busy. She ignored the pain in her hip. She'd become the master at ignoring pain over the past winter after her life blew up in her face last year.

Roxanne threw a grin her way when Shana reached the counter. "Coffee?"

At Shana's nod, Roxanne turned away to get the coffee ready. Roxanne was a close friend and the owner of the store. She quickly filled a takeout cup and handed it to Shana. "Morning run?" she asked.

"Yup. Not my best plan. It's slick in the shady areas, and I slipped. I figured I'd rest for a few here before I head back home," Shana replied.

"I'd offer you a ride, but I'm the only one here so far." Roxanne's eyes broke away from Shana and beyond Shana's shoulder. "Hot damn! Any idea who that is?"

Shana turned and almost choked on the sip of coffee she'd just taken. Her pulse rocketed. Hayden Thorne was walking into the coffee shop, a man she certainly didn't expect to see. Her belly clenched, and heat raced through her body.

Hayden slipped a pair of sunglasses off, his caramel eyes meeting hers. A hint of surprise was reflected in his, the only thing giving her a tiny glimmer of relief. He walked toward her, his stride long and powerful. He was tall and lanky with hair that almost exactly matched his eyes.

"Hey Shana, nice to find a familiar face right away," Hayden said.

Her face was hot, but she managed a nod. In the brief silence, Roxanne cut in. "And who would you be?"

Hayden's eyes shifted to Roxanne. He took a step closer to the counter. "Hayden Thorne. I'm here for a visit from Montana. I met Shana last year when she came out there."

Understanding dawned in Roxanne's gaze as she nodded. "Right. Welcome to Catamount. I'm Roxanne. You found the perfect place to stop, seeing as you just got to town. Can I get you some coffee?"

"Coffee would be perfect," Hayden replied with a smile. "Nice to meet you, by the way."

"Ditto," Roxanne said with a grin as she turned away. She quickly served Hayden a cup of coffee and started to speak when another few customers stepped up to the counter. Roxanne glanced to Hayden. "I'm a bit too busy to chat now, but stop by anytime." Her eyes bounced between Shana and Hayden. "Maybe you could give Shana a ride home. She took a tumble on her morning run."

Shana flushed and silently swore. Roxanne could sometimes be a tad too perceptive and was never one to hesitate to interfere. Before Shana had a chance to respond, Roxanne swung away, immediately jumping in to take the next customer's order. Shana pasted a polite smile on her face when she turned to Hayden.

"No need to give me a ride. I was stopping to take a little break before I finished my run." She tried to quell the zing of electricity in her body when Hayden's eyes landed on her.

"I don't mind. I have no idea where I'm going anyway. You can help me with directions." Before she could reply, Hayden continued. "Did Dane mention I was coming out here for a visit?"

No, her older brother most certainly had not told her. But then, Dane and most of her friends continued to try to keep her in a bubble when it came to anything that had to do with the mess her late-husband, Callen Peyton, had left behind. Hayden Thorne was a mountain lion shifter from Montana who worked for the Feds. He'd been a big help when she'd bolted out there last year to unravel the secrets Callen had left hidden until his death on a highway on Connecticut. A mountain lion getting hit by a car on the highway in Connecticut was news no matter how you sliced it. Eastern mountain lions had been considered extinct for half a century though rumors swirled that they still lived.

Callen's death had burst onto the news because it was the first confirmed sighting of a mountain lion in the East in over seventy-five years. Only Catamount shifters knew the truth. Mountain lions had evolved to become shifters—shifting back and forth from lion to human at will. Catamount, Maine was one of their strongholds in the East. Shana came from a long line of shifters and had married Callen Peyton because it seemed like everyone thought she should. If only she'd listened to her heart, she wouldn't have felt like such a fool when she found out Callen had gotten in deep with a drug smuggling network and started trying to find ways to sell the services of Catamount shifters to the highest bidder. His efforts led to his death after a ridiculous attempt to demonstrate shifters could safely navigate in lion form through the busier parts of the Northeast.

"Shana?"

She swung her gaze up to Hayden, swearing to herself. She'd completely zoned out in front of the one man who seemed capable of thawing the ice around her heart.

"Uh, no. Dane didn't mention you were coming for a visit." She scrambled to say something else though her capacity for casual conversation appeared to have temporarily left her. She pushed away from the counter and went to move toward a table. Her step lurched when she tried to put weight on her injured hip.

Hayden took a step toward her. "Looks like you could use that ride. How about..."

She cut him off. "I'm fine, just a little slip on the ice." Her hip throbbed its disagreement, but she ignored it.

Hayden's eyes coasted over her, assessing. He looked as if he was about to say something else until he met her eyes. Whatever he saw there changed his mind. "Even if you're fine, falling on cold pavement sucks."

Shana's heart thumped—hard. A ride home would be lovely and far more comfortable than trying to run three miles mostly uphill to get back home.

"Oh, right. Um, sure. A ride might be good. It's slicker out this morning than I thought."

She figured if she refused the ride, it would make more waves than if she went along with it. Hayden glanced around, his eyes assessing the room. He took a swallow of coffee. He exuded a quiet, watchful power and strength. Damn if he wasn't knee-weakening sexy. His eyes, like hot caramel, landed on her again.

"Shall we?" he asked, gesturing toward the door.

Shana nodded and began to walk toward the front of the store. Hobble was the more accurate term. Despite her best efforts, her hip was stiff and tight, throbbing with pain from its collision with the pavement. When she reached the door, Hayden stepped to her side. His hand slipped around her back, his touch burning hot.

"Take it easy," he said, his voice low and warm. "You insist you're fine, but I'm not so sure. Should I take you...?"

She cut him off, waving her hand dismissively. "No, no. I don't need to go anywhere but home. It was a hard fall, but a hot shower is all I need."

Her voice sounded shrill to her. *Great, just great. You sound like a cranky bitch. Well, lately I have been a cranky bitch. How about you cut me some slack?* Her inner critic slouched to the corner. She couldn't quite think about the fact that she hated how she felt lately. Two of her closest friends had found love recently. Happy as she was for them, and she truly was, a tiny corner of her tattered heart wanted to scream and stomp its feet. Maybe she hadn't loved Callen—though no one, not even her closest friends knew that—but she'd tried to make their marriage work for the sake of... Who was she kidding? For the sake of her pride and Callen. She'd been too embarrassed to admit the marriage had turned into an utter sham. When he died, she'd been stunned. She had genuinely been sad at first because, even if she didn't love him the way she thought she should have, she had cared for him and never wanted to see any shifter die after getting hit by a car. Such an undignified death, a travesty for a majestic creature. But then, Callen's secrets spilled out for the world to see. Now, she had to face the shame of not knowing what he'd been doing and somehow move on with her life.

She'd thrown herself into helping with the investigation into Callen's drug smuggling and gone to Montana in search of Callen's connections. Months ago, Callen's father had been arrested, along with his brothers and a few other accomplices. For all intents and purposes, Catamount had moved on.

Meanwhile, her heart had felt encased in ice for years. The moment she laid eyes on Hayden in Montana, the ice cracked. He was like no one she'd ever encountered. He was tall and lanky with a deceptive strength. He carried himself almost lazily, but she'd seen him in action. As a mountain lion, he took her breath away. As a human, he sent her heart racing and heat unfurling through her veins. She'd come within a breath of kissing him in Montana. She had told no one about her unannounced visit to his office one afternoon in Montana. Thinking about it now suffused her with liquid heat. She remembered his eyes, burning into her, his lips, inches away. Before he swore and stepped back, his eyes shuttering. He was a man of honor. That she knew. He respected her brother and wouldn't dare take advantage of her. Bitterly, she considered he probably thought her weak and needy because of what happened.

Her mind returned to the present, Hayden's palm warm on her back, his other hand cupping her elbow. She'd convinced herself her recollection of the heat she felt with Hayden in Montana was an overblown figment of her imagination. But now, with him near, she wondered if she'd underestimated it. Somehow, she kept it together while he walked her to a black sports utility vehicle and helped her inside. The vehicle was blessedly warm.

Hayden turned to her. "Where to? The only directions I have are to Dane's place."

"Lucky for you, I live in the guesthouse on Dane's property."

He arched a brow. "Oh? Okay then. We'll just let my GPS tell us where to go then. You can let me know if there's a quicker way."

"What brings you out here? Last I heard, things were mostly resolved with the smuggling network in Catamount."

He nodded as he slowly pulled off the side of the road. "That's what I've heard from Jake and Dane. Problem is, things are still running hot out in Montana. Dane suggested maybe I could get some info from the guys here sitting in jail while they wait for their cases to go to court. The federal prosecutor in Montana is working with the office in Portland to see if they can work out a deal if these guys will help us out on the other side."

"Oh. Well, that makes sense. I hope you can get somewhere with it." Hayden almost passed the entrance to Dane's house. "Hey, turn..."

His GPS intoned its instructions just when she started to speak. He caught her eyes and chuckled before slowing and turning abruptly.

Shana took in the familiar landscape as they drove down the winding lane leading to the estate. Dane lived in their childhood home, which was an old colonial farmhouse, stately and lovely. After Callen died, it was all she could do to even walk in the home they had shared. Dane and his new fiancée, Chloe, had offered to let her stay with them in the main house, but Shana needed privacy. She'd moved into an old renovated barn, which had been converted into a modern guesthouse.

She directed Hayden to the guesthouse, a

good mile away from the main home. He parked the car and leapt out. Before she had a chance to move, he was opening the passenger door. She started to move, too fast for her stiff hip, and gracelessly fell against him. Hayden's arms caught her easily. Her eyes slammed into his. Time stopped. Her pulse quickened, her breath became shallow. The pull she felt toward him was so strong, she was powerless to resist.

He froze in place, though she could feel his heart pounding where her breast mashed again his rock-hard chest. His eyes darkened and flicked to her mouth. With thought impossible, she acted on instinct, lifting her free hand and stroking it through his golden brown hair and down along his cheek, savoring the rough stubble. His breath hissed before his lips crashed against hers. The ice inside her melted into liquid heat pulsing through her veins, twisting in her core. His lips feasted on hers, his tongue diving in, sweeping through her mouth. Her tongue tangled with his as she pressed closer, desperate for the heat he offered, the intense feeling he stoked inside of her.

Sensation prickled along her skin, slivers of fire. Wet heat built between her legs, and she shifted restlessly. Finally feeling something after so long was so unbelievably good, she could hardly stand it. It didn't help matters that Hayden kissed like no other. Soft and slow, rough and fast—the combination drugging her senses, taking her breath away, making her want more and more. He abruptly tore his lips away.

She wasn't ready for him to move yet, and he didn't. He hooked an arm on the doorframe, his breath coming in gusts against her cheek. She closed her eyes, savoring his warmth, his strength. Sensation pinged low in her belly, warm and sweet. She almost sobbed in relief. After the emotional chilly years of her marriage and trying to adjust to Callen's death, her emotions had dulled. She'd so desperately wanted to know she could feel again and now she did.

"I shouldn't have done that," he said, his voice tight.

She opened her eyes to find his trained on her. His pulse beat visibly in his neck. "I started it," she whispered. "It's okay."

For a second, she thought he might kiss her again, but he slowly straightened. Her eyes flicked down and saw the bulge in his jeans. She resisted the urge to stroke him through the denim. She couldn't help the tiny thrill of knowing she had an effect on him.

"Maybe so, but I know you've been through a lot this year. You don't need me acting like an idiot." He took a step back. His mouth curled up in a wry smile. "You're so damn beautiful, it makes it hard."

She tried to recall the last time any man had called her beautiful. Callen had largely ignored her the last few years, her self-esteem draining slowly away. He'd never been the most attentive man, but once the newness of their marriage wore off, Callen had carried on his life as if she was a mere afterthought. If he had a priority for their relationship, it was that they kept up the social image of a happy couple. Bitterly, she considered how his actions had torn his social image to shreds after his death. She batted the memories away and met Hayden's eyes. She couldn't help her return smile.

Shana's slow smile nearly undid him. He had to yank the reins of his control to keep from kissing her again. *Fuck.* He was in serious trouble. He'd conveniently forgotten how insanely tempting Shana Ashworth was with her glossy honeyed locks that fell in waves halfway down her back, her smoky silver eyes, and her sensual, full mouth. Adding to the temptation, her body was all lush curves and strength. Hayden had spent his life around mountain lion shifters. Female shifters were renowned for their beauty. Shana took it to another level, primarily due to her natural sultry manner and complete obliviousness to how delectable she was. He recalled meeting her in Montana and being relieved he'd been seated at a table. He respected her brother and knew she'd been through a lot, so it absolutely wasn't okay for him to be battling a hard on every time he got near her.

When she mentioned where she lived, the wheels in his brain started spinning. Dane had said Hayden was welcome to stay in the guesthouse. Dane couldn't have meant for him to stay with Shana. Hayden was ashamed to admit the idea took his mind down the paths of some wild fantasies. The kiss just now had set him on fire inside. But he couldn't go there.

Hayden came to Catamount to see if he

could find a chink in the armor around the shifter smuggling network in Montana, not to get caught up in fantasies about Shana Ashworth. He glanced back at her, and her smoky eyes nearly shredded his control. He took a breath and another step back.

Shana's eyes broke from his and she started to climb out of the car. Her breath hissed, her face barely tightening, when he recalled there was a reason he'd ended up with her in his arms. She was hurt.

He moved swiftly, carefully sliding his arm around her. She went stiff, but she didn't shove him away.

"Let's take it slow," he said.

He felt the deep breath she took. Glancing down, her expression was controlled. She nodded quickly.

"Right. Slow seems to be the way to go. I didn't realize how hard I landed." Her voice was husky and sounded surprised.

Though Hayden couldn't say he knew her well, he sensed her to be a woman who rarely showed weakness. Her brother had intimated as much when he talked about his worries about the effect of her husband's death and the trail of misdeeds he left behind for her to clean up. Hayden wanted to know her, wanted to peel back the brittle layers around her, and find the woman he sensed underneath. Which was insane.

They made it inside the guesthouse. Shana limped inside. He had to force himself to ease his grip on her. His body didn't want to move away. He wanted to pull her close again for another kiss. When she turned to face him, lust jolted through him. He held still, trying to force his body under control.

Her silver eyes met his, the corner of her mouth kicked up. "I didn't think I needed a ride, but obviously I did. Thank you."

"No problem."

"How long will you be visiting?"

He shrugged. "Not too sure. At least a week or more."

She nodded, her eyes thoughtful. "Well, I'm sure I'll see you again. I'm supposed to have dinner with Dane and Chloe tonight. Where are you staying?"

A flicker of heat flashed through him. The mere thought he might end up staying anywhere near her set his pulse racing. "Not so sure. Dane actually mentioned staying at the guesthouse, but I'm assuming he means another one."

She flushed and bit her lip. *Holy hell.* She

needed to *not* do that. It brought his focus right to her lips and nothing else. Now he knew what they felt like under his, well that wasn't particularly helpful for getting his body to cool down.

She shrugged and rolled her eyes. "He probably meant here. Dane, uh, well he conveniently forgets to mention some things to me, especially if they have anything to do with my late husband. We never would have met you if it hadn't been for everything Callen set in motion, so Dane was probably worried about telling me you'd be here."

Hayden's heart tightened. He didn't know what to say, but he knew it must be painful for Shana to come to terms with the man her husband had been.

She saved him from having to formulate a reply. "It's fine for you to stay here. There's plenty of space. There's a separate apartment on the other side. Why don't you go on over to Dane's and check in with him? I'll probably see you tonight at dinner."

Moments later, Hayden pulled to a stop in front of a lovely old farmhouse another few minutes down the road. His brain was fuzzed from his encounter with Shana. He grabbed a water bottle and splashed the cold water on his face, the activity jolting his brain off of Shana. He wiped his face with a towel and climbed out of the car. Somehow, he had to get his focus on why he was here. Though if Dane truly intended for him to stay in the guesthouse, even in a separate apartment, his will was about to be tested to the max.

2

Shana stared at her reflection in the mirror. The face looking back at her appeared weary, or perhaps that was her interpretation because that's how she felt most of the time lately. Before Callen died, her life hadn't been amazing, but it had been stable and predictable. Well, as stable and predictable as life for a mountain lion shifter could be. She'd been born and raised in Catamount, the town founded centuries ago by her family and a few other shifter families. Catamount was mid-sized and bustling now, busy spring through fall with tourists trekking up to Maine for a taste of "The Way Life Should Be," the official state motto. The Appalachian Trail meandered its way through Catamount, so the town was host to many hikers and others. Though Maine relished its reputation for having protected its wilderness better than many eastern states, it made money hand over fist with tourists. Catamount catered to them with high end shopping, arts, and plenty of restaurants. The only thing they didn't have was their own ski lodge, although there was one in a neighboring town.

Little did those tourists know they were surrounded by mountain lion shifters. Shana had grown up steeped in the lore of her family and absorbed the belief she would marry another shifter. When Callen Peyton started flirting with her in college, he seemed exactly the shifter she was expected to marry. He came from another founding family and was handsome and popular. Though Shana didn't feel too much of a spark with him, he was attentive and charming at first. She couldn't quite come up with a reason not to marry him, so she did. At thirty-one years old now, looking back on their marriage through the knowledge of the man Callen really was, she saw what she couldn't see then—a young woman uncertain of her place in the world who wanted to please her family. If only she'd had the courage to say she wasn't ready.

By the time Callen died, Shana had given up thinking she could find a way to make their marriage better. They hadn't been intimate in almost two years. She knew he had casual dalliances with women on his many trips out of town because he didn't bother to hide them from her. He was careful never to have affairs with anyone local because image mattered to him, and he wanted to keep up the image that they were happily married. She had been working on building the courage to tell her friends just what the truth was when he died. Only then had she learned how little she knew about his life.

With a sigh, Shana turned away from the mirror. She'd had just about enough of introspection lately. Walking through the bedroom, she grabbed a scarf off her dresser and slung it across her shoulders. After Hayden had dropped her off this morning, she'd called Dane. He hedged and acted as if he'd 'forgotten' to tell her Hayden was visiting.

She mentally armored herself and headed out the door to dinner. After a hot shower, the pain had eased in her hip enough she could walk with only a slight limp. Her body was taut with anticipation at seeing Hayden again, while her mind swung wildly between self-doubt and recrimination. She didn't know when there was a 'right' time to be open to anything resembling a relationship, casual or more, after one's husband died. Were there rules for this and were they different if your husband hadn't touched you in years and any semblance of love had been long gone?

HAYDEN LEANED BACK in his chair, carefully keeping his eyes from landing for too long on Shana. He'd spent the day with Dane and Jake, mostly reviewing what they'd learned over the course of their investigation in Catamount. Dane planned to take him to the police station tomorrow. In the meantime, Dane and Chloe insisted on inviting him for dinner. Shana joined them, and Hayden became deeply aware of how weak his control was when it came to her. All she had to do was sit across the table from him, and his body hummed to life.

Chloe turned to Hayden with a smile. "So

Hayden, when does the snow melt in Montana?"

Hayden shrugged. "Sometime between April and June."

Chloe grinned. "That's about the same answer you'll get around here. This is my first spring in Maine, so I feel foolish thinking the snow should be gone for good by March. I suppose it's about the same in most of the northern states."

Chloe was lovely with golden hair and forest green eyes, yet Hayden felt absolutely no spark with her. Which was good because Dane would probably tear his throat out if he did. Hayden only considered Chloe in contrast to the effect Shana had on him. After dropping her off this morning, she'd sauntered through his thoughts here and there throughout the day, but he'd mostly convinced himself his reaction to her was overblown. Then, she'd walked into her brother's house for dinner. It was as if a match lit the air between them, a flame licking its way across the room.

Hayden chanced a look in her direction. She swirled a glass of wine in her hand, the deep red of the wine matching the scarf draped across her shoulders. Her hair glinted under the lights. Her silver eyes tilted up to meet his. Lust tightened inside. She swung her gaze to Chloe with a smile.

"Spring may come late up north, but it's that much sweeter for the wait," Shana said.

Chloe angled her head to the side. "I suppose so. I almost did cartwheels the other day when I saw the daffodils blooming."

Dane slid his arm across her shoulder and leaned over to drop a lingering kiss on Chloe's cheek. "I told Chloe we'd have to bring the old greenhouse back to life," he said, his eyes catching Shana's.

Shana smiled softly in reply, her gaze wistful. "Have you used it at all since Mom passed away?"

Dane shook his head. "Nope. Kept meaning to get around to it, but gardening was never my thing."

Chloe grinned up at him. "I've already made plans for next year." She glanced at Hayden and stood. "You must be tired after that long flight." She turned back to Dane as she circled the table, gathering plates and silverware. "Did you get the extra apartment ready for Hayden over at the guesthouse?"

Dane shrugged. "Nothing to get ready." He turned to Shana. "Would you mind showing Hayden the guest apartment over there?"

Shana nodded, her expression controlled and unreadable. Hayden had purposefully steered clear of asking Dane outright if he'd be staying in the same guesthouse where Shana was. Though it appeared he'd be in a separate apartment, his body kicked up a notch from its state of high idle at the mere thought of being in proximity to Shana. He must have blanked out how flat-out sexy Shana was before he'd planned this trip. His mind had been solely focused on the on-going investigation into the shifter smuggling network in Bozeman, Montana. He'd been relieved to learn Catamount had taken down Wallace Peyton and his cohort. Hayden still didn't think the source of the network was in Bozeman, but it was wreaking havoc among shifters in the area. Factions were drawing lines within the shifter community. Some shifters had even fallen prey to addiction while others gloried in the quick influx of cash. Hayden hoped he'd find a few trails to follow after he had a chance to talk to the shifters here. In the meantime, Shana's presence was a temptation he hadn't even considered.

He needed to get a handle on himself because he didn't need Dane to pick up on his feelings. Dane was understandably protective of his sister after what she'd been through over the last year. Hayden had been nothing beyond polite with Shana in Dane's presence, so he could only hope Dane hadn't noticed anything else. Dane followed Chloe into the kitchen. Hayden took a deep breath and stood to help finish clearing the table. The mundane activity brought his focus away from Shana. By the time she walked into the kitchen a few minutes later, he firmly had the reins on his control.

SHANA LED the way down the granite walkway toward the entrance to the additional guest apartment in the old renovated barn. Hayden followed a few feet behind her. As promised, she was showing him the small apartment where Dane had offered for him to stay. The entrance was on the other side of the barn from where she stayed. Her heart pounded in time with each step she took. Over dinner, she'd come to a decision. The effect Hayden had on her was like nothing she'd ever experienced. She was tired of sticking to the script she thought she should follow—the one that involved her acting only when she thought her choices would be approved by others. That had gotten her nothing but a cold marriage to a man whose lies went far beyond their marriage. Hayden would come and go, so it wouldn't matter if she had a fling with him. She didn't know what anyone else might think of her choice, but she didn't care.

Since Callen's death, she felt more trapped than she'd felt when he was alive. Now, she had to carry the burden of his betrayal, in addition to the weight of their failed marriage. By the end of it all, she'd felt like half a woman. She couldn't recall the last time a man had noticed her until she'd met Hayden out in Montana. She'd thought it was a fluke, perhaps all in her head. Until this morning when she'd kissed Hayden. She had a taste of what it meant to feel something again, and she was determined to have more.

So she decided she would let herself have something—Hayden specifically. The only question remained was whether he'd allow it. After their kiss, she believed he wanted her, perhaps even as much as she wanted him. But she didn't know if he'd allow his misguided honor to get in the way.

She reached the door and quickly turned the key in the lock. Flicking the lights on, she gestured for Hayden to come inside.

"Here you are," she said, swinging her arms around the room.

Hayden took a few steps inside and turned in a circle. Though it was small, the space was lovely. The original plank wood flooring had been finished to a shine. An efficiency kitchen was to one side of the room with the rest living space. A tiny woodstove painted bright red sat in the corner with a couch and matching chairs overflowing with pillows nearby. An alcove at the back held the doors to the bathroom and bedroom. The remaining door led into the area where she was staying. She gave Hayden a tour in less than three minutes.

When they stepped back into the central area, Shana shivered. She glanced to the woodstove. "We need to get you some wood in here. Let me check to see if the propane stove works. Dane may have forgotten to check on that."

She fiddled with the controls on the

small propane heater. "I think we're out of luck." She glanced up at Hayden who stepped to her side. He proceeded to do just as she'd done and shrug.

"Suppose I didn't need to bother seeing as you just did that," he said with a chuckle.

"Let's get you some wood from my place. I have plenty stacked inside."

She stepped a little too quickly, her stiff hip hobbling her for a moment.

"Easy." Hayden's low voice sent shivers through her. His hand curled around her arm, the touch sending ripples of heat outward through her body.

Her breath caught, but she held still. Much as she wanted him, she wasn't as brazen as she'd like to be because she hesitated.

His eyes met hers, banked heat in them. His gaze was like warm brown sugar sliding over her. She forced herself to breathe and nodded towards the door that led into her apartment.

His eyes swung to the door and back to her, a question in them.

"Come on. Right through here." She broke free from his soft grasp and stepped to the door. Another turn of the key, and they walked into her apartment. Warmth seeped through her. The chilly air outside was cold enough to leave a spring frost on the ground. Flicking on a few lamps, she made her way to the far side of the apartment by the entryway where she kept wood stacked in a rack by the door.

Suddenly, she stopped and whirled around, almost colliding with Hayden who was right behind her. Her heart battered against her ribs. She focused on the flicker of heat Hayden had set to life inside of her. It made her remember she had the capacity to feel passion, to feel anything, again. She gathered the tattered remnants her courage and met his eyes. He was a tall man, his presence strong and almost hulking. His tawny gaze held hers. When she couldn't find words, she followed her body's lead.

Only inches separated them. She closed the gap and slid her palm up his chest, savoring the flex of his muscles under her touch. His heart beat strong and sure as she coasted over it. His breath hissed between his teeth when she stroked up his neck and threaded her fingers in his hair.

Hayden opened his mouth to say something, and Shana tugged him down to meet her lips. The initial point of contact sent a jolt of sensation streaking through her. His muscles flexed under her hands and then he moved swiftly, stroking a hand up into her hair and the other sliding around her waist to tug her against him. She gasped at the feel of him. His tongue dove inside. Their kiss went wild. He stroked deeply into her mouth before gentling his touch, tracing her with his tongue and nipping at her bottom lip before diving in again. She'd meant to take control and found herself awash in waves of longing, drugged by his overpowering presence and the feel of him against her. His arousal was hard against her hip.

He stroked roughly through her hair, angling her head back as he tore his lips from hers. They blazed a hot, wet trail around her ear and down her neck, sending hot shivers coursing through her. His palm slid up her back, a path of pure heat and strength. She arched into him, frantic to get closer. Longing surged through her, so deep it shook her to her core. Too long without any intimate touch, she'd wondered if she'd lost the capacity to feel passion. With Hayden, she came afire in his arms.

His lips and tongue meandered in slow,

tortuous path along her collarbone, dipping down to the valley between her breasts. He started to tug at her blouse when he froze completely. His lips left her skin, and he lifted his head. His warm amber eyes met hers. Her pulse beat so rapidly, she could barely catch her breath. It felt as if they were suspended in time, hot, liquid need pulsing between them, an otherworldly passion shimmering in the air around them.

He looked almost pained. He swallowed, easing his grip slightly. He cleared his throat. "Shana, you have to know I want you. So much." His voice was rough, barely above a whisper, the sound itself shimmying under her skin, amping up the sensation coursing through her. "I don't know if this is such a good idea. Your husband..."

Anger arced through her. She shook her head sharply. "My husband not only wasn't the man I thought he was, he hadn't touched me in over two years when he died. Our marriage was a joke."

Hayden's eyes widened, sadness and confusion passing through them.

She took a shaky breath. "No one knew what it was like. Before he died, I was trying to get the courage to divorce him.

When I met you in Montana, it was the first time in years I felt something. After wasting too many years of my life the way I did, I don't want to do that anymore. I barely know you, but I know what I feel between us. I don't have any expectations. I just don't want to be the good girl anymore. I want a chance to feel something again. If you're worried it will get complicated, it won't. I know you enough to guess you might worry about my brother. Don't. I'm far past needing him to take care of me. It's none of his business."

She ran out of words and remained still. To say aloud what her marriage with Callen had really been was such a relief, emotion tightened her chest for a moment before loosening with the release of the secret. Her eyes fell, landing on the golden skin at Hayden's throat. The collar of his shirt was open, revealing just enough skin to tempt her. She knew by touch that he was all muscle under there. Desire raced through her, ebbing and flowing with each breath and beat of her heart.

"Shana." Hayden's voice was low, taut and vibrating with feeling.

She met his eyes again. Her low belly

clenched, wet heat pulsed between her thighs.

"I'm sorry."

For a moment, she thought he was saying he was sorry, but he couldn't be with her. Shame began to rise inside of her. Mortified that she'd dredged up the courage to approach him, she questioned if she misunderstood what she thought she felt from him. She started to pull back, but he held her firm, a hand tightening on her hip while the other slid around her back. His eyes held hers, searching.

He shook his head slowly. "No, I'm sorry for what your marriage was. You didn't deserve that, no one does."

Relief eased the tension rising in her. For all her bravado in practically launching herself at him, she was suddenly shy. To have the truth of her life out there made her feel too exposed, too vulnerable. After a year of one train wreck after another, all the while trying to keep her chin up, the weariness started to edge its way into the moment.

Hayden's eyes held hers expectantly. She pulled the words up out of her. "No, no one deserves that. It's made everything that happened over the last year...complicated."

He nodded slowly. "It was complicated to begin with, but yeah, I'm guessing that made things even harder for you."

Silence fell again. He still held her close. His heart beat against her hand. The heat of his palm on her back anchored her. Desire pricked at her. She didn't want the truth of her life to interfere with what she felt. She needed to *feel*, to just *be,* she needed the escape his touch offered.

She idly traced the edge of his collar, his skin warm under her touch. His breath came out in a sharp gust. Whatever he thought, his body couldn't lie. The heat of his arousal was still evident, a hot brand against the edge of her hip. "So?" she asked, her voice coming out rough.

His eyes, those eyes she could lose herself in, burned into her. "You're right that I might have worried about what Dane thought. Not because I think Dane has the right to say anything about who you're with, but because I didn't want to take advantage of you."

"You're not. I am grieving what's happened, but not the way you maybe thought. I grieved my marriage for years. Since Callen died, I've had to come to terms with how many levels of his life were a lie. But don't think for a minute you're taking advantage. If you respect me, don't let your decisions include what my overbearing brother might think. I'm far past needing his protection. I want this, I want you."

Hayden held still, the silence between them weighted, before nodding once. He didn't say a word. He simply tightened his fingers in her hair and fit his mouth over hers again.

3

———

Shana's silvery eyes looked up at his, a mix of sultry, sexy, and vulnerable at once. Hayden hadn't quite recovered from learning her husband had ignored her. How any man could ignore Shana was beyond comprehension. She was breathtaking and nearly wrecked his control just by existing. A tiny corner of his mind reminded him Dane would probably disagree emphatically with Hayden's choice to accept what Shana was offering. But then, Hayden's honor here was to Shana, and she was right to argue her brother had no say in this part of her life. She'd lived through a grueling year and done so mostly alone since, if he understood correctly, no one close to her knew she'd been living in a loveless marriage.

While he could tell himself this was happening because it was what Shana wanted, the truth was he wanted her with such force, he could hardly corral his feelings. He heard the words "I want this, I want you," and the drumbeat of his heart rose to a crescendo. Her hair was like silk. He tightened his loose grip on it, crashing his mouth to hers again.

Her mouth opened instantly, her tongue tangling with his. He tugged her closer, groaning at the feel of her lush curves against him. He slid a hand down to cup her bottom, savoring its fullness, the give under his grip. She arched into him, pressing against his arousal. Lust surged through him in waves, crashing so hard and fast he could hardly think. But he wasn't going to let her go through a rushed coupling after years of nothing. He wrangled control of his body and tore his mouth away. His breath came in ragged gasps, but he would slow this down if it killed him.

"Bedroom?" he choked out.

Her eyes had gone smoky. She met his, heat thick between them. She nudged her head behind him. He turned, grabbing her hand. When he felt the hitch in her step, he paused and lifted her against him. Her breath came out in a soft puff, and then she giggled. Her giggle nearly broke the thin thread of control he'd latched onto. In the times he'd seen her, he couldn't have imagined her giggling. The sound of it reached in and grabbed his heart.

He strode quickly toward the door he presumed to be her bedroom, shouldering through it to find himself in dark room. His eyes adjusted to the dimness. He could make out a large four-poster bed against the far wall. Shana flicked on a lamp as he carried her across the room. She giggled again when he knelt and carefully set her down. Every inch of him had to fight against the urge to roughly take her. A tiny corner of his mind kept reminding himself she'd fallen this morning.

Casting his eyes around, he reached over and flicked on another lamp by her bed. Her bed was piled high with pillows. She fell against them, her hair in a tousle around her face, her smoky gaze pinned to him. He stood swiftly and kicked off his shoes before turning his attention to her. He slipped her flats off and paused to catch his breath. She wore a gauzy skirt that hugged her hips and twirled at the bottom. He slid his hands up her calves, savoring the strength of them. Her breath caught, sending another jolt of lust through him. He leaned on his knee and brought himself to rest at her side. Stroking a hand in her hair, he commenced to taste every inch of her.

Kissing her was like diving into sweet madness. She threw herself into it—hot, wet, drugging kisses, her tongue tangling sinuously with his. Over the next span of time, Hayden lost all sense of anything beyond the moment to moment between them. He forced himself not to tear her clothes off right away on the erroneous assumption it would help him maintain control. Instead the taunt and tease of feeling her curves through her silky blouse and gauzy skirt notched the heat so high inside, he could barely breathe.

Desperate, he finally tore at her blouse. The buttons slid loose through the silk, revealing her breasts barely covered in black lace. Her breath came in pants and gasps, shredding at his control. The next few moments were a blur as he mapped her body with his hands. Her breasts were lush and full, her nipples dusky. She was all curves and strength, flexing and writhing under his touch. He dragged her skirt off and stroked a finger across the wet silk between her legs.

He paused to look up at her long enough that she lifted her head, her smoky eyes locking with his. Somewhere along the way, she'd shoved his shirt off. His pants were unbuttoned, barely containing his cock, which pulsed at the mere thought of being inside of her.

"Hayden..." Her voice came out on a breath and curled like smoke through him.

He stroked the silk again, satisfaction surging through him when her hips shifted against his touch. He set a steady rhythm of strokes, increasing the pressure of his touch, until she was arching into him. Only then did he drag the black lace out of the way, tossing it across the room, and bringing his mouth to her. A low moan came from her as he set to know this part of her. He stroked through her folds with his tongue and fingers, slowly sliding one and then another into her channel. Her hips were restless, her cries broken between her gasps. He felt the build up inside of her, her channel tightening and pulsing around his fingers. She rocked her hips against his mouth. When her entire body went taut, he sucked her clit into his mouth. She tightened and went still before shudders wracked her body. When her hips settled again, he drew away and stood.

SHANA LAY DAZED, pleasure spinning through her. All she'd wanted was to feel again, and Hayden had gone and driven her far past any point of pleasure she ever could have imagined. She was tossed in the tumult of sensation. She dragged her eyes open to find him kicking his jeans to the side of the room. Bare, he was a sight to behold, all lean muscle, every inch of him molded and sculpted. He bore faded scars on his chest. Shifters tended to fight and play hard when in mountain lion form and often bore the scars of it. He held a condom in hand and efficiently tore it open, rolling it on in one motion. She'd known by feel that he was well-endowed, but to see him almost took her breath away.

The mattress gave under his weight when he placed a knee on the bed. He moved fluidly, his heat surrounding her as he rested atop her. His elbows bracketed her face. She had wanted this more than she'd known. Yet, she'd been entirely unprepared for the intimacy between them. Because she'd never had the taste of such a feeling. Desire shimmered around them. When his heated gaze met hers, her breath caught in her throat. Her body was pliant from the orgasm that had just crashed through her, but the moment she felt him against her, she was desperate for him to fill her.

He brushed her tangled, damp hair away from her face. His heart beat against her breasts. Liquid need coursed through her. He let his hips fall against her, the weight settling in the cradle of hers. His cock rested against her sex, soaked with want. She felt like she should speak, but she couldn't form words. She arched against him. In the quiet, taut moments that followed, he slowly ground against her, his cock sliding back and forth against her, nudging her higher and higher into the acute pleasure.

"Shana, I'm trying to go slow..."

His voice broke. She dragged her nails down his back and arched roughly against him, breaking his control. He plunged into her, the surge rough and deep. She almost sobbed in relief at the fullness. Her body clenched around him, unused to being stretched and filled. He held still for a long moment until the tension eased from her. Then, he set to slowly driving in and out of her, his control absolute as he set a steady rhythm. Pressure gathered, tightening its coil inside of her. She curled her legs around his hips and arched up to meet him. This orgasm was even more intense, starting in slow, sweet pings of sensation that built and built until it crashed through her in almost violent waves. Only when she cried out, scoring his back with her nails did his control break. His hips pounded into hers before his entire body tightened and he arched back with a cry. He held still, his head hanging forward, his weight resting on his arms.

Their breath echoed in the room. He slowly eased down, resting to one side of her. She didn't want him to withdraw, wanted to maintain the connection, every inch of him as close to her as possible. Her breath finally slowed. He stroked a hand through her tangled hair, his other hand resting on the curve of her belly. She didn't know how much time passed when he spoke.

"It's getting cold." His voice was gruff and

broke through her reverie.

She rolled her head to the side and met his eyes. They held a question. While their communication was remarkably good without words when they were skin to skin and caught in the heat between them, she wasn't up for guessing just now.

"What?" she asked.

He was quiet for a moment before speaking. "I'm not sure if you want me to stay, or if I should make my way out."

Though a corner of her mind warned against it, she didn't care to listen to the voice of 'should' anymore. It hadn't done her much good up to this point in her life.

"Stay here. As it is, if you don't start a fire, it will be freezing in there by morning. If you're worried about Dane, I'll just tell him there was no heat and you stayed in one of the bedrooms here. All of it will be true," she offered, a giggle escaping.

It occurred to her she hadn't laughed much at all recently and definitely hadn't giggled. Hayden affected her in more ways than she could have imagined.

His mouth hooked in a smile. "No argument from me. I'll need to go grab my bag though."

4

———————

Hayden woke to the feel of Shana's warm, soft body curled up against his. Her bed was ridiculously comfortable with a soft down quilt encompassing them in weightless warmth. It was early yet, the wispy light of dawn filtering through the sheer white curtains. When she shifted in her sleep, his body came to instantly, his cock hard in seconds. Shana had ruined him last night. Oh, he'd wanted her since the moment he'd laid eyes on her last winter in Montana. He'd chalked it up to nothing more than wanting a beautiful, sexy woman who had an aura of unattainability due to the circumstances of her life at the time, or what he'd thought them to be.

Now, in the cold light of morning with last night fresh in his mind, he was left to consider just what the hell he was going to do now. There was *no way* he could say no to her if she wanted him, but he didn't know what she wanted. He recalled her brief, flat statement about what her marriage had actually been. Callen's involvement with the smuggling network and the betrayal and lies he set in motion were nothing compared to what he'd done to Shana. Hayden wasn't a fool. Though he had experience with a serious relationship, he'd never married. He knew from watching other friends go through the trials and tribulations of long-term relationships that what you saw on the outside most certainly didn't reflect what lay between two people. To learn Shana had married Callen because she thought she should and he'd gone on to ignore her sliced through Hayden. Shana wasn't a woman to ignore. For Shana to have had to face Callen's betrayal against the shifters on top of what he'd already done to her infuriated Hayden.

Hayden turned his head to look at Shana. Her tawny hair fell across the pillows. Her thick lashes rested against her cheeks. Her plump lips were pink and still swollen from his kisses last night. He couldn't resist and leaned over to kiss her. Despite his body's disagreement, he forced himself to keep it light. When he pulled away, her eyes opened. Her silvery gaze met his, and his heart clenched.

"Morning," he said.

A slow smile spread across her face. "Morning." She rolled over to glance at the clock on the nightstand. Rolling back over, she slid her foot up and down his calf. Lust surged through him.

"We should get up. What time were you and Dane meeting today?"

"We didn't really say."

Hayden seriously did not want to get up. He wanted to stay right here in the tangle of Shana and lose himself in her. He also seriously did not want to have her brother knocking at the door in the middle of it.

"I suppose we should get up, huh?"

Shana giggled and nodded. She wiggled away from him and climbed out of bed. He enjoyed the glimpse of her luscious body as she walked into the bathroom adjoining the bedroom.

A while later, after he'd been pleasantly surprised by Shana's call for him to join her in the shower, Hayden walked out of the bedroom. While he'd have liked a much longer interlude than he'd just had, his body was in check after Shana twined herself around him in the shower.

He glanced around her apartment. The guesthouse was a renovated barn, a massive building. The main entrance into this living space was comprised of double doors that swung open into a charming area. Colorful throw rugs were scattered over hardwood flooring. The front part of the barn had been turned into a living room, dining area and kitchen with shiny stainless steel appliances and light spilling in from many windows. The upper portion of the barn was left open with the old hayloft reached by a spiral staircase and containing shelves of books on the walls with a small sitting area. Roughly halfway into the barn, a hallway led to Shana's bedroom and another across the hall. The door at the back led into what Hayden knew to be the small apartment intended for him to use. He wondered if he would stay there at all. Half of him thought perhaps he should, while the other half of him vehemently disagreed, thinking he needed to get every possible moment he could with Shana until he returned to Montana.

Coffee scented the air. Shana poured him a cup and got started making omelets. As he was digging into a delicious spinach and feta omelet, there was a sharp knock at the door before Dane stepped inside. Shana quickly glossed over her decision to invite Hayden to stay in this part of the guesthouse, making the plan sound final.

Hayden held his breath, wondering if Dane would pick up on anything between him and Shana. In lion form, it would be all but impossible for Hayden to hide his feelings from Dane. He had a chance in his human form. Hayden didn't particularly feel he needed to hide anything, but he respected Shana's choice to keep her privacy. If this with her were nothing more than temporary, it would likely stay that way.

Yeah, and you know damn well you're already way past thinking this is temporary. His mind taunted him with the knowledge of the intimacy between him and Shana last night. It was unmistakable. He just hadn't had a chance to process it. He was still trying to wrap his brain around the fact that it happened.

~

LATER THAT MORNING, Hayden followed Dane into the police station. He glanced around the old building. He'd quickly noticed that Maine was filled with old homes turned into something else. Something else could be anything from a renovated home, a storage facility, a business, or a local government building. Catamount's police station was housed in an old colonial building. Dane knocked quickly on a door and stepped through.

"Hank, this is Hayden Thorne, the guy from Fish & Wildlife out in Montana. Remember how I mentioned he planned to visit to chat about our investigation?"

Hank was an older man, weathered and lean, with the clear look of a shifter. He stood and came around his desk, holding his hand out.

"Hank Anderson, chief of police here in Catamount. I spoke to one of your cops out there last week. We're hoping we can help out, but it'll depend on the guys we arrested being a little more helpful."

Hayden nodded. "Right. I'm glad you guys were willing to talk options. Any word from the prosecutor on whether they'll strike a deal if we get some help on intel for the Montana end of things?"

Hank nodded. "They're open to it. You know the drill though. It'll all depend on how much they talk and if it's actionable information."

Conversation moved on with Hank scheduling a few meetings for Hayden with the prosecutor handling the cases. He'd already reached out to the attorneys for the clients in question to obtain permission for Hayden to interview them. After that, Dane took Hayden down to check in with Jake.

Jake's eyes were glued to a computer when they walked in. He didn't even look their way. "Hey guys, have a seat," Jake offered distractedly.

Hayden sat down in the chair Dane gestured to. He recalled Jake to be the computer whiz who'd traced Callen's contacts to Montana. Hayden wished they had somebody half as good as Jake in their area. He was hoping

Jake would be willing to do some extra work now that they'd shut down the smuggling network in Catamount for the time being.

Dane caught Hayden's eye. "This is Jake when he's on his own turf. He hardly ever leaves here. It used to be worse, but he finally got a clue and shacked up with Phoebe. Now, he has a reason to go home," Dane said wryly.

Jake tossed a balled up piece of paper at Dane's head as he swiveled away from his computer. "Hey man, good to see you," he said with a nod to Hayden. "How are things in Montana?"

"If you're asking about the weather, it's great. Spring's on the way. If you're wondering how things are with the smuggling network, not so good. They've made a few arrests, but it's pretty entrenched out there. I'm hoping maybe some of the guys here will think it's worth talking and know something worthwhile."

Jake shook his head and sighed. "Right. I'm hoping for the best. I thought maybe if you could go over anything new you have, I'll do some online digging for you."

"You read my mind. I gotta say, the police out there have some guys that do what you do, but you seem to have the magic touch."

Dane chuckled. "It's safe to say, if Jake wanted to go rogue and hack into networks and steal money, he'd be rolling in the cash."

Jake rolled his eyes and brushed his light brown hair out of his eyes. "You guys had lunch yet?" he asked as he stood.

"Nope," Dane replied.

"In that case, let's head over to Roxanne's. I need coffee and food. Phoebe had an early morning shift at the hospital, so I didn't even have coffee and breakfast at home."

Hayden followed Dane and Jake outside into the cool spring morning. The spring frost was melting as the sun's rays struck the ground. Hayden glanced around as they walked several blocks down the street. Catamount had a timeless quality to it. The town was tucked in the foothills of the Appalachian Mountains. Unlike out West, the mountains were right here, not hulking in the distance. He curiously read the small painted signs in front of some of the homes, denoting when the home was built and by whom. Many homes were several centuries old. They reached a lovely town green surrounded by a granite stonewall with granite paths crisscrossing through the center of the green.

Hayden was reminded of Catamount's age in relation to many of the communities out West. Among shifters, Catamount was legendary. It was known as the birthplace of mountain lion shifters. While wild mountain lions had managed to keep a healthy population out West, the situation became dire in the East hundreds of years ago. If mountain lions hadn't developed the ability to shift, their very existence would have been threatened in the East. As it was, they were considered extinct in this part of the country. Shifters gradually spread through North America, intermingling with wild mountain lions and humans. Among the wild population, they were considered superior due to their powers. Hayden had plenty of reason to come to Catamount to follow up on the smuggling network investigation, but he'd been drawn to visit out of pure curiosity to see the place where shifters came into their power. His own family ancestors originally came from Catamount a few generations back. Shifters had purposefully spread out in the hopes to prevent mountain lions anywhere from ever facing the danger Eastern mountain lions had. Humans would be stunned beyond belief if they knew just how many shifters lived out in the open amongst them.

Hayden followed Jake and Dane into Roxanne's Country Store. When he'd stopped here the other day, he'd been drawn by the cheery sign and bright blue door, along with his need for coffee after the long flight from Montana. The front portion of the store had groceries and other odds and ends. Jake led them through the aisles to the back area, which opened up to a deli and coffee shop. Tables were scattered around, most filled. When they approached the counter, Roxanne grinned at them.

"Hey boys, what'll it be today?"

Her bright blue eyes met Hayden's gaze. "Nice to see you again."

Dane chuckled. "Roxanne, this is Hayden..."

She waved a hand, her blonde ponytail swinging when she glanced between them. "We met yesterday when he stopped here for coffee."

Dane's brows hitched up. He caught Hayden's eyes and gestured to Roxanne. "Roxanne's family is one of the founding families of Catamount. Roxanne inherited this store from her grandfather. If you need local information and gossip, Roxanne's is basically the center of the universe in Catamount." Turning back to Roxanne, Dane continued. "If you recall, Hayden was a big help to us out in Montana. We're hoping we can return the favor now."

Hayden would have guessed Roxanne was a shifter, but Dane's point that her family was one of the founding families of Catamount confirmed it. Shifters everywhere lived by a code of silence. Aside from a hunch, shifters only confirmed themselves to others if it was known to be safe. Roxanne turned her broad smile to him again.

"I heard plenty about how much you helped these guys after they got back from Montana. I hear the smuggling network is still running out there though."

Hayden nodded. "Unfortunately. It's been pretty well established there for a few years now. I don't know if we can ever completely wipe it out because that kind of thing is like a peat fire. It can burn underground for years and pop up every so often. I'm hoping to have better luck maybe taking down some of the big players though."

Roxanne nodded firmly. "Of course. In the meantime, welcome to Catamount. Be careful though, you just might want to stay. You know what they say about Maine."

Hayden's puzzlement must have shown on his face because Roxanne clarified. "The way life should be. That's the state motto."

Hayden chuckled, his mind wandering to Shana. Maine was lovely, but not near as lovely as Shana. He forced his mind away from Shana and nodded at Roxanne. "I can see why. It's beautiful here."

"Anyway, what can I get for you guys?"

After a delicious cup of coffee and a hearty sandwich for lunch, Hayden leaned back in his chair. Dane and Jake were casually discussing some of the leads Jake could chase down in Montana. Hayden felt a prickle on the back of his neck and turned to find Shana walking toward their table. His body instantly tightened. Her tawny hair was loose around her shoulders. Phoebe Devine, Jake's fiancée walked at her side, her eyes only on Jake. Shana's silver eyes met his briefly. He felt the air between them come alive. Damn. He was going to have to call on every ounce of his reserve control to keep it together around her. All he wanted was to stand and bend her over one of the tables and take her—right here, right now.

That most certainly was not an option. She wore fitted leggings and boots, the leggings hugging the curves of her legs and hips. A flowing purple blouse with a scoop neck revealed the tops of her generous breasts. Hayden's cock twitched. He breathed deeply, forcing himself to look away from her.

When they reached the table, Shana hung back. Phoebe leaned over to kiss Jake. Jake didn't hesitate to slide his hand into her dark curls and tug her in for a proper kiss. By the time Phoebe pulled away, her cheeks were flushed.

"How many times to I have to remind you two to tone it down?" Roxanne's sly question came over Hayden's shoulder.

Jake grinned while Phoebe flushed even deeper.

Roxanne clucked and refilled their coffees before moving on. Phoebe met Hayden's eyes.

"Good to see you. How was your flight?"

"Uneventful," he offered with a smile. "How have you been?"

Conversation carried on with updates offered all around. Shana kept quiet, but her presence couldn't be ignored. Not by his body at least. Every tiny movement she made caught his eye. He was thankful to be seated at a table because otherwise his arousal would be easily obvious. He only hoped he could will it away before it was time to stand.

5

————————

S hana watched the landscape roll by as she rode in the passenger seat of Phoebe's car. Phoebe had stopped by after her shift at the hospital and persuaded Shana to go into town for a few errands and lunch at Roxanne's. Shana hadn't expected to see Hayden there, and his presence had thrown her. Somehow, this morning had felt light and dreamlike. She'd woken in his arms, awash in sensation. While she'd known she wanted him, she hadn't known what it would be like to actually experience intimacy with him. He'd transported her beyond any place she'd ever been and left her sated.

Instead of waking to doubts, she'd felt

lighter than she had in years and hadn't even worried about trying to explain away his presence to Dane. The hours in between had sent doubts racing to the forefront of her mind. All she'd wanted was to feel again. She'd thought Hayden would be safe. He lived halfway across the country. He was the perfect candidate for a fling. She hadn't counted on how her heart would respond. Her body came alive and her heart called to her to listen to what it wanted. What was supposed to be just sex was so much more with Hayden. For certain, the sex itself was beyond intense. Somewhere in the midst of the deepest sexual experience she'd ever had, her heart clamored, convincing her Hayden was meant to be hers.

She knew her shifter self well, but she'd never quite gone for the whole 'mates who were destined to be together' idea that floated amongst shifters. Then, she'd never met a man, even in passing, who called to her the way Hayden did. If her shifter had any say in the matter, she'd follow Hayden to the ends of the earth to hold onto him. And that scared the hell out of her. Even in her fear, what gave her pause was the plain truth that if she'd listened to her shifter side before she'd married Callen, the marriage never would have happened. The doubts had simmered and she'd carelessly ignored them and paid dearly. Now, when faced with the depth of her shifter's feelings about Hayden, she didn't quite have the courage to follow her heart just yet.

"Shana? Are you with me here?"

Phoebe's voice cut into her thoughts. She swung to look at Phoebe who'd come to a stop at the guesthouse where Shana was staying.

"Huh?"

Phoebe arched a brow. "Did you hear anything I just said?"

Shana flushed and shook her head.

Phoebe unbuckled her seatbelt and grabbed her purse. "I asked if I could borrow your old sewing machine. Mine broke yesterday. I've repaired it so many times now that I think it's time to move on. You never use that old one your mother gave you, so I hoped you wouldn't mind if I borrowed it until I get a new one."

"You can have it for all I care."

Phoebe grinned and climbed out of the car. "Let's get it now."

Shana led the way inside and headed for

the large storage closet in the hallway. After getting the sewing machine out, Phoebe set it on the kitchen table and started looking it over.

Shana's chest felt like it was going to burst. Being here, thinking about what happened with Hayden last night made her desperate to tell Phoebe the truth about her marriage. Phoebe was her closest friend. Shana had never quite understood why she'd felt the need to hide the truth about Callen from Phoebe, but she'd been so embarrassed.

Phoebe was engrossed in checking the settings on the sewing machine when Shana blurted her secret out.

"When Callen died, we hadn't slept in the same bed for two years."

A pair of scissors clattered to the floor when Phoebe's hand fell to the table and hit them. Her dark eyes met Shana's, confusion swirling in them.

"What?"

"Just what I said."

"You and Callen hadn't slept in the same bed in two years before he died?"

Shana nodded, relief loosening her chest.

"What does that mean?"

"It means our marriage was a lie. Callen

never loved me. I keep trying to remember the last time we had sex, but I can't. I know it was more than two years before he died. He had affairs whenever he traveled. I know because he never bothered to hide them from me." Shana paused, her throat tightening, bitterness welling with her pain.

When Callen died, she was sad, truly she was. Because even though their marriage was a disaster, she'd believed he cared for her as she cared for him. The past year had been a living hell as his betrayal ran through the ranks of shifters in Catamount and eyes turned to her in suspicion. She wished upon wish she'd told her closest friends how bad things had been between them, so she could make sense of how she felt. But there had been too much happening, and she couldn't even think clearly.

Phoebe stood from the chair at the table where she sat and wrapped Shana in a hug. "Oh honey, why didn't you tell me what was going on? I'm so sorry. All this time, I've been worried you were trying to come to terms with what he'd done, but it was more than that." She pulled back, her eyes bright with tears. "Two years? Callen was a fucking asshole. He never deserved you. Never. I was not his biggest fan, but you know that. I had no idea it was as bad as it was though."

Shana's tears flowed freely now. She nodded jerkily. "I know you didn't exactly adore him, but you tried to be good about it. I should have said something, should have divorced him. But I thought my parents wanted me to marry him. They were so excited about the whole founding families joining together thing. It wasn't so bad at first. I never knew it could get as bad as it did. When he died, I'd been trying to work up the courage to talk to you about it and maybe even divorce him. Then, everything blew up. I'm so tired of hiding it, so I had to say something."

Shana swiped at her tears. Phoebe swung away and stepped to the kitchen counter. Snagging a napkin, she handed it to Shana. After she wiped her eyes, Shana took a shaky breath.

"So there, that's all I had to say. It felt huge, but there really wasn't much to it," she said. A knot of pain and bitterness that had been coiled tightly in the corner of her heart finally unwound, a sense of relief and openness rushing in its place.

Phoebe watched her carefully. "It was

huge. Is it something you want anyone else to know?"

"I don't know. I'm so tired of Dane tip-toeing around me, maybe it'd be good if he knew. I don't want to spread it far and wide because it's embarrassing, but I don't want to act like I had this amazing marriage with Callen either. Honestly, things were at the end when he died. I feel awful for how he died. Even with everything he did, I hate what happened to him. I really do. It's just such a mess."

Shana sat down with a thud in the chair beside Phoebe, twisting the napkin in her hands. Phoebe was silent for a moment.

"Should I make some coffee or tea? Better yet, how about we have an afternoon happy hour?"

Shana couldn't help but smile. Phoebe would sit right here with her all day and night if that's what Shana needed.

She glanced at her watch. "It's already four. It's safe to have a glass of wine and not call ourselves lushes."

Phoebe grinned. "Absolutely!" She swung away again and grabbed a bottle of red wine out of the wine rack and brought it, along with two glasses, to the table. After she poured them, she held hers up for a toast.

"Here's to moving on."

Shana took a gulp of wine and set her glass on the table. "You have no idea what a relief it is to have that out there!"

Phoebe nodded. "I can guess. The last few years have been hell for you, and I didn't even know how bad it was until now."

"I suppose one way to look at it is things can only get better."

Phoebe shrugged. "Maybe so. You know, I'm calling Jake to ask him to pick me up later. I don't want to have to worry about how much I'm drinking. Maybe we should call Roxanne and Lily. I'm all about laying this out all at once. What about Chloe too?"

Several hours later, Shana glanced around at her friends. Roxanne was arguing with Chloe over what she should put in the greenhouse, while Lily and Phoebe were cleaning up in the kitchen from the impromptu dinner they'd had. Shana hadn't wanted to turn this into an event, but she was more than relieved she could stop glossing over the truth of her former marriage with her closest friends.

Dane, Jake, Hayden and Noah Jasper entered the room. Dane was there to collect Chloe. Jake was there to pick up Phoebe as promised. Noah Jasper was there for Lily, Jake's younger sister. Looking around, Shana giggled when she realized how their small circle just kept pulling more people into its orbit. She was beyond happy for her friends though her heart felt a sharp pang when she considered her own situation.

Roxanne got busy organizing who was riding with whom. Meanwhile, Shana's eyes wandered to Hayden and her breath caught in her throat. Her pulse quickened when his caramel eyes landed on hers. She was relieved everyone else was busy getting jackets on and not paying the slightest notice to her and Hayden. Because if they had been, she couldn't imagine they wouldn't notice the electricity arcing to life between them. Even across the room, she could feel his presence. Her body started to hum. She physically had to resist the urge to walk over to him.

Long moments later, the bustle around them faded. Only Phoebe was left. Jake had carried the sewing machine out to his truck while Phoebe finished putting her jacket on. She looked over at Shana and then to Hayden. Her gaze narrowed, but she didn't say anything. She walked to Shana's side where her hips rested against the kitchen table.

Phoebe gave her a quick hug and whispered in her ear. "That man wants you. In case you didn't notice." Her eyes held a wicked glint when she pulled away.

Without another look back, Phoebe strode across the room and out the door with a wave to Hayden. Silence fell in the room once the door closed behind Phoebe.

Hayden stood by the kitchen counter, his hands in his pockets, eyes locked on her. The air felt alive, snapping with the heat of their attraction. Only a look from him, and her mouth went dry and she struggled to catch her breath. Her belly fluttered, desire tightening in her center. She felt the moisture between her thighs, instantly craving his touch there, anything to relieve the intense longing.

In slow motion, he pushed away from the counter, his hands sliding out of his pockets. A few long strides and he stood before her, the heat and strength of him almost vibrating. The air around them came to life. Shana's entire body tingled with need. His shoulders rose and fell with a deep breath. She could see his pulse beating in his neck, strong and steady.

"We didn't talk about what's next. You said there wouldn't be any expectations. But what if there's more to this than that?" he asked, his voice gravelly.

Her pulse ran wild. Hope crashed through her. A hope she had long ago written off. If her cat had her say, she already knew there was far more to *this* than something casual with no expectations. But she was unprepared and not quite ready to know what she felt. She knew she was long past any romantic grief over Callen. That had gone years before he died. What she felt with Hayden was on another map entirely—one she hadn't known existed. She not only had no directions, she didn't even have a compass to navigate the emotional, sexually charged playing field between them.

She took a breath and tried to gather her thoughts with her pulse pounding and desire surging through her veins. "If there's more to this than that, we'll figure it out." Her voice came out raspy.

HAYDEN WATCHED SHANA, wrestling to keep hold of himself. Her honeyed hair fell in disarray around her shoulders, her silvery eyes had gone smoky, and her lips were so pink, so inviting. He heard her words and tried to compute them. He wanted to push, to demand more. Any moment his mind had been free today, his thoughts had wandered to her. On a primal level, he knew she was meant to be his. Yet, the time to push wasn't now. So, he accepted what she was willing to give.

He closed the distance between them, threading his hands in her hair and fitting his mouth over hers. In a flash, the low burn he'd carried inside all day soared to a wildfire. He slid one palm down her back to cup her bottom, so soft and full, and tugged her against his arousal. Her mouth opened on a gasp, and he swept his tongue inside. Lust pounded through him. Their kiss scorched him through. His cock strained against his jeans. He didn't know if he'd be able to hold back tonight.

She flexed into him, soft whimpers coming from her throat. He tore his lips away, needing to taste her skin and trailing a hot, wet path down her neck. He savored the shivers that wracked her. He tore at her blouse. It rent against his rough touch, revealing what he supposed was a bra, a concoction of purple lace barely holding in her generous breasts. Glimpses of dusky pink peeked at him through the lace. He closed his mouth over a nipple, right through the lace. She arched into him, gasping. He soaked both of her nipples before flicking his thumb under the tiny clasp that held her bra together. Her breasts tumbled out.

Shana slid her hands under his shirt, shoving it up and over his shoulders. He leaned back just far enough to pull it off his head and fling it across the room. She yanked him to her. The feel of her skin, soft and damp with passion, notched his need higher. Her nails scored his back. Her lips, teeth and tongue mapped his chest, nipped at his neck. Her hands got busy unbuttoning his jeans. When she slipped her hand inside his briefs and curled her palm around his cock, his head fell back on a groan. She pushed him back and knelt before him. In a blur, she shoved his jeans and briefs down around his hips and took him in her mouth.

Hayden nearly came right then and there. He scrambled for control and hung on just barely. The warm, wet heat of her mouth nearly undid him. She was slow and fast, rough and soft at once. She licked up the length of him, cupped his balls lightly in her hands, and teased him to the very edge of his endurance before she drew him fully inside her mouth, taking him to the hilt. He choked out her name and yanked her up. He stroked his hands roughly down her sides, cupping her breasts for a moment on the way down. His hands kept traveling, hooking over her leggings and panties at once to shove them down. Desperate only to be inside of her —*now*—he turned her, fumbling in his pocket for a condom.

$\sim$

SHANA TURNED and braced her hands on the kitchen table. She felt the velvety heat of Hayden's cock brush against her cleft. She was beyond desperate, soaked with want for him. She heard the sound of foil tearing. Her anticipation climbed. She pressed back into his hips, soft pants and gasps breaking from her throat. He slid his knee between her thighs, pushing them apart. He stroked into her folds, roughly delving inside her channel. It wasn't enough, only drove the need to have him fill her higher.

"Not enough..."

Her words came out between ragged breaths as she arched back into him.

"I need..."

"This." He bit out as he surged inside of her, sinking in to the hilt. She cried out, almost sobbing in relief. One of his hands gripped her hip as he began to thrust in and out of her. The other slid up her back in a hot stroke before threading into her hair and pulling her toward him with each surge inside of her. Her channel throbbed around him. She was so close, so near the edge that she raced to the release. His hips pounded into her, rough, deep thrusts. While she arched into him, her hips pushing back to meet his again and again. She tumbled into the chaos of pleasure. It spun loose, sensation barreling through her. He slipped his hand around her front, instantly finding her clit and exerting just enough pressure that she screamed when her orgasm finally hit her. As she clenched and throbbed around him, he drummed his hips into her, his own cry following hers.

The table and Hayden's strong grip on her hip were the only things holding her up. Bowing her head, she tried to catch her breath. He slowly released his grip on her hair. After several long moments, he slowly eased his hips back. She instantly missed the fullness inside of her. She pushed her weight up on her hands and turned. His touch never left her. He simply followed her turn, his hands sliding around to rest of her hips again as she leaned against the table.

She lifted her eyes to his and blinked at the intensity she found there. She knew it was reflected in her own gaze, but it didn't change how startled she was. What she'd meant to do was give herself a chance to have something, to feel something, with someone she thought could be easily kept in a compartment. Hayden was anything but that. He was everything she wanted even though she hadn't even known what she wanted. After Callen, she'd have been perfectly content to have a few flings, but never planned to commit to anyone. That would have suited her. The peace had been something she craved. *This,* this electric, otherworldly, all-encompassing feeling was beyond her understanding.

Her cat nudged at her consciousness, the one part of her that did understand. She took a breath. His warm gaze slid over her before his hands fell away. "Shower?" he asked, his mouth hooking in a small smile.

She nodded, a smile blooming in her heart, her lips following suit. She sensed he may have wanted to say more, but he held back. For that, she was relieved. She knew there would be a point where she couldn't keep this at bay, and perhaps they'd already passed that point, but for now she wasn't quite ready to look too closely at what lay between them.

6

———————

Hayden turned when the door to Jake's office opened. Noah Jasper stepped inside. Hayden had met Noah the day before and learned he'd been instrumental in the local investigation into the shifters here. Noah was to bring him to the county jail to meet with his uncle, Theo Jasper. The Jaspers had relatives in Montana, namely Carl Jasper, who'd led Jake to Theo.

Jake was deep into whatever he was doing on his computer and barely nodded at Noah's entrance. After a long silence, Noah turned to Hayden.

"You'll get used to this with him," Noah offered, gesturing to Jake. "He ignores pretty much everything and everyone when he's working."

Jake chimed in. "I'm working, I'm not purposefully ignoring everyone." He turned away from his computer and smiled sheepishly. "In fact, I managed to chase down a few email aliases on some of the new names you brought me from Montana." He hitched his brows up when he glanced Noah's way.

Noah chuckled. "No one doubts you're not productive."

Jake's teasing manner disappeared. "Noah's gonna take you to the county jail. Theo's his uncle, so he might have more pull getting him to cooperate with you."

"Theo might be my uncle, but we were never close. Theo takes care of Theo. He was low on the totem pole here in the investigation, so he figured he'd play it smart and turn the others in. He doesn't exactly have many friends. As far as what he knows about things on the Montana end, hard to tell. He's not stupid though. He won't make shit up because that'll boomerang on him. If he's got intel and thinks it might shorten his sentence, he'll probably talk."

Hayden nodded. "I figure I'll talk to anyone who'll talk to me. The police out there are up to their ears in petty arrests. They'd like to nab someone other than low hanging fruit."

Noah nodded and stood. Jake caught his eyes as he did. "Where's Lily today?"

"Home working. You know her, she's a lot like you. Buries her head in computer code and comes up for air only once in a while. She said she wanted to have you and Phoebe over for dinner soon."

Jake nodded. "Just tell me when." He shifted gears. "Call me with an update after you guys talk to Theo."

At that, Hayden and Noah exited Jake's office. Noah offered to drive, and Hayden took him up on it. Catamount was in the northern portion of its county, so they headed south through the mountains. Noah was comfortable with quiet, which Hayden appreciated. Hayden took in the scenery as they headed south and pondered what it would be like to shift here. While in some ways it was safer out West since mountain lions roamed wild out there, in others ways it was more dangerous. In some areas, hunting was legal, so shifters had to be doubly careful during hunting season. Since Eastern mountain lions had been on the decline for over a century before they were declared extinct, the species had been protected for decades. If anyone happened to encounter a shifter lion in the woods, it would serve as a tall tale, but was otherwise harmless for shifters.

The road wound through the hills. Hayden's mind wandered to Shana because anytime he wasn't entirely focused on something else, that's where his thoughts went. He couldn't quite believe he'd woken a few days ago in Montana without Shana in his consciousness. His brief interactions with her when she was in Bozeman had been memorable, but he hadn't gotten close enough to realize the depth of the spark between them. After a mere two nights with her, his entire being pulled in her direction anytime she was near. Though his lion side knew what he felt with her was far beyond what he'd expected after the first night, he'd half talked himself out of it before last night. Today, he didn't even bother to try to talk himself out of it. He'd thought nothing could compare to the first night. Now, he reflected it was more that no one could compare to Shana. If he let his lion enter his feelings at all, he couldn't imagine walking away from her. But he knew she wasn't sure.

Though his conflicted feelings about her grief over her late husband's death had morphed after understanding what their marriage had been, it didn't change the fact that she'd been through a difficult year. Her life had been turned upside down in more ways than one. As for him and what he wanted—he wanted Shana. Completely. Though he hadn't planned for this and had no idea how to get to that point, he would find his way.

He considered his life in Bozeman. While his grandparents had moved there from Catamount, his own parents had moved away when he was young. He'd spent most of his childhood in Colorado, another stronghold for shifters. His parents had died in a car accident on a snowy highway in the Rocky Mountains shortly after he graduated from college. With his grandparents also dead, he had little to anchor him anywhere. He'd followed his degree in biology into a position with the Feds at Fish & Wildlife in Colorado and accepted the transfer to Bozeman when it came up. Yet, the one thing he lacked was a sense of home. Without close family to tether him somewhere, he often felt out of place.

As a shifter, given that he had to hide half

of his being from many people he encountered, he'd have loved to have the connections he observed here in Catamount. It
wasn't just among family, but among the
shifters in general. He could see why the
smuggling network had torn at the fabric of
this community. The role Catamount held in
the shifter world was sacred. To have shifters
betray each other here, of all places, was
painful to consider. He tried to envision
bringing Shana to Bozeman, but it didn't
quite fit. He wasn't sure how he'd go about it
or when, but he sensed if he meant to make
her his mate, he'd have to relocate his life to
Catamount.

Noah's voice broke into his thoughts. "Almost there. Theo's pretty easy to understand.
He's rough and tumble and always looking
for easy money. He got into the smuggling
network for the cash. No other reason. He
talked because he was smart enough to realize they might make him the fall guy."

"Right. Sounds like half the guys involved
out in Montana. Money makes a bad friend,
but shifters are as dumb as people
sometimes."

Noah smiled wryly. "True."

Several long hours later, Hayden walked

at Noah's side through the parking lot. In silence, they climbed into the truck, and Noah started driving. Hayden was stunned. Among other things, Theo had dropped a bomb in his lap—the name of Hayden's boss at Fish & Wildlife, Clint Reynolds. Though Theo was short on details, he reported Clint was rumored to be running the show in Montana. Hayden thought of the many, many conversations he'd had with Clint over the last few years about the shifter smuggling network. Clint avoided any tedious work, thus his delegation of most duties associated with coordination with the local law enforcement didn't seem unusual. It wasn't that Fish & Wildlife officers handled much law enforcement, but they often got involved in issues relating to management of lands. With the smugglers frequently attempting to access remote areas for deliveries and other purposes, Fish & Wildlife was called in repeatedly for assistance. Clint conveniently bowed out every time, now that Hayden considered it.

He glanced over at Noah. "Not sure you picked up on it, but Clint Reynolds is my boss and the regional director of Fish & Wildlife in our area. The fact that Theo even knew his name makes my stomach turn. You got Jake's number? It never occurred to me to ask him to take a look at Clint."

Noah quickly recited Jake's number. After calling Jake and putting him onto Clint, Hayden leaned back with a sigh. He was too mentally worn out to think much more about the smuggling network.

SHANA SAT at Phoebe's kitchen table and poured cream in her coffee. Phoebe wiped her hands on a dishtowel before stepping to the table and slipping into the chair across from her. Phoebe's house, now shared with Jake, was like a second home for Shana. She'd stayed here for a few weeks after Callen died and had spent more evenings with her friends here than she could count.

Phoebe sifted her hands through her dark curls and tied them into a knot atop her head. Her dark eyes assessed Shana. "What's up with you and Hayden?"

Shana tried to hedge, panic edging her thoughts. If her feelings were so obvious, how could she protect her heart? "What do you mean?"

Phoebe rolled her eyes. "So that's how you're going to play this? Whatever. I think you finally decided to talk about what your marriage to Callen was actually like because maybe meeting a man who really is interested in you made you think it wasn't worth pretending anymore. I saw the way Hayden looked at you the other night. I'm surprised he didn't go up in flames."

Phoebe had never been the friend to shy away from anything, but sometimes she was so spot on, it made Shana squirm. Shana opened her mouth to speak, but Phoebe held a hand up.

"The look on your face confirms what I was thinking. I don't know exactly what's between you and Hayden, but there's a little more there than a fun roll between the sheets. You need to know maybe none of us knew you and Callen were married in name only by the end, but I wasn't blind. I noticed things weren't exactly great. I just figured you were trying to make it work anyway. If you're worried about what people think, don't. You deserve something good after everything you've been through."

Tears pricked Shana's eyes, and her throat felt tight. She'd cried so much this past year, it annoyed her. She took a breath, willing the tears away, and met Phoebe's eyes. "Doesn't everyone deserve something good?"

Phoebe angled her head to the side and smiled ruefully. "Well, sure. But that wasn't my point. Even if Callen hadn't died and hadn't betrayed you and the rest of Catamount shifters, you'd have every right to move on, to find someone who appreciates you. It helps a bit that Hayden's hot as hell and clearly thinks you are too." She winked at that.

Shana blushed and absently twisted a napkin in her hands. "I'm not going to argue that point. I just...ugh. I don't know what's supposed to happen right now. All I wanted was..." Her words trailed off.

She didn't know how to explain that she'd been desperate to *feel* again after the numbness she'd cocooned herself inside to get through the last few years of her marriage. She held onto that numbness like a lifeline after Callen died. When Hayden showed up, he was like a candle flickering in the cold, dark night. She'd only wanted to follow the flame, to let it melt the ice around her heart. But being with him was so much more than she'd expected. She recalled his question the other night—hinting at how to handle the reality that there was clearly more between them than a fling with no expectations. She'd underestimated the fire between them. It burned so hot and fast, she was afraid she'd get singed in its heat. After the utter failure her marriage had been, it was hard to believe anything good could last. It wasn't to say she had experienced anything with Callen remotely like what she felt with Hayden, but she'd never have known their marriage could go cold, bitter and distant in a few short years. Which made it all the harder to think beyond temporary with Hayden. To feel what she felt with him and face the possibility of it fading and withering was terrifying.

Shana met Phoebe's eyes again. "I don't know what to do. For God's sake, don't mention it to Jake because he'll tell Dane, but Hayden and I...well..." Flushing madly, she shrugged.

Phoebe grinned. "Got it. No need to explain. Great news as far as I'm concerned. Why do you look so worried?"

"Because it seemed perfect. Hayden doesn't even live here. As you pointed out, he's pretty easy on the eyes and definitely notices me more than Callen ever did, even before we were sleeping in separate bedrooms. But...it's, um, a little more than I expected and I'm not sure what to do."

Phoebe's eyes sobered. She reached over and squeezed Shana's hand quickly. "What does Hayden have to say? If anything."

Shana chewed her lip and took a breath. "Before anything happened, I told him I wouldn't have any expectations. I didn't want to have any. Later, he asked what we would do if there was more to it than that."

Phoebe nodded slowly. "Well, it's not like I know Hayden all that well, but his question leads me to think he might be thinking it's more than he expected too."

Hope twirled in a small circle in her heart. Shana tried to tamp it down. Her breath came out in a sigh. "Right. I'm worried I can't think clearly because I'm so desperate for something good. Just a tiny dollop of it and I'm getting too excited. Hayden doesn't even live here. It's not like I can..."

Phoebe waved her hand. "Oh stop it! I want to be supportive, I really do, but I'm not gonna let you start going in crazy circles in your mind. Trust me, I'm an expert at that and it's a complete waste of time. It's always easier to tell other people to do the things I couldn't, but I'm telling you now—stop. Don't tie yourself up in knots over things that haven't even happened."

Shana giggled, recalling how twisted up Phoebe had been over Jake for years. Her heart loosened the tiniest bit as she recalled some of her own advice to Phoebe. Matters of the heart were so much easier to interpret when they didn't involve one's own heart. "Fair enough. So what should I do now?"

Phoebe burst out laughing. "Try to relax and focus on now. I'm here. I'm always here for you, so if you need to obsess or talk anytime, you know exactly where I am."

7

───────

Late that afternoon, Shana stood at the edge of the woods. The sun was low in the sky, its rays angling through the trees, dappling the ground with its light. The early spring air held the earthy scents of new growth. She needed to run free and temporarily forget the vagaries of her human mind and emotions. On the heels of a deep breath, she shifted. Energy coursed through her, whipping from head to toe. Her fur rippled across her skin. She held still for a moment, her mountain lion's eyes adjusting to the forest. She stretched into her form, sighing at the feeling of strength and power. Another breath and she dashed into the woods. The far end of her family's property extended into the foothills of the Appalachian Mountains. She started off at a run, but once she got deeper into the mountains, she slowed to a jog.

The forest was alive with sound. Birds returning from their southerly migrations flitted busily among the trees. A pair of chipmunks chattered loudly at her when she passed by. She kept her pace, jogging slowly through the woods, winding further up into the mountains until she reached one of her favorite places, a small hillside that looked out over a valley, a stream meandering lazily through the valley. She rested atop a boulder. The sun had begun to dip lower in the sky. Its golden rays were shot through with orange and red.

Suddenly, she lifted her head, scenting another mountain lion nearby. Several moments later, the lion in question came into view just below her in the valley. She stared for long moment until the lion looked up. Instantly, she knew it was Hayden. He was bigger and bulkier than most of the male mountain lion shifters in the East, likely due to the reality that shifters out West had much more freedom to roam in the wild out there. His eyes met hers across the distance. He turned to face her, his tail flicking. From a complete standstill, he bounded forward, his motion fluid and seamless. In seconds, he climbed the small rise where she waited and came to a stop beside the boulder.

Up close, he was magnificent in cat form —pure strength, power and vitality. Her cat nearly purred at the sight of him. Deep inside, the pull to him was so strong, so intense, she quivered. The connection between them stitched tighter as he stood there, his caramel eyes locked to hers. She stood and stretched on the boulder and leapt down to his side. The air was alive around them. In the quiet, she turned and began weaving her way back down the mountainside. When they crossed into a field, she broke into a run, pounding across the distance. Hayden stayed on pace with her. She gloried in the feel of the air through her fur, the freedom from her human confusion. Here and now, she knew only one thing—she wanted Hayden and no one else.

HAYDEN RACED ALONGSIDE SHANA, pulsing with energy and primal desire. He hadn't known he'd find her out here. He'd returned to the guesthouse this afternoon to find it empty. He'd been unsettled and out of sorts ever since the interview with Theo at the jail. Trying to wrap his brain around the fact that the truth of the power behind the smuggling network might have been sitting under his nose every day in the form of his boss made him sick. He sought the escape and freedom his lion offered and had followed a worn footpath to the edge of the forest behind the guesthouse. Once out of view, he shifted and took off. It didn't take him long to catch the scent of another lion ahead of him. He immediately knew it was Shana, so he followed her trail until he found her.

He glanced sideways. She ran at his side. She was breathtaking in her cat form, lithe and sensual. When they reached the edge of the trees, she shifted back into human form. He followed. The light was fading, the air chilly. He turned to see her already gathering the clothes she must have left behind. He followed suit, though it almost caused him physical pain. As he glanced around while they walked back to the guesthouse, he realized they were in full view of Dane and Chloe's home. He wryly considered it probably wouldn't be the wisest plan to take Shana under the circumstances.

She was quiet as they walked. Her hair fell in disarray around her shoulders, her breath misted in the air. When they stepped into the guesthouse, she turned to him. Her smoky eyes held his steadily. He considered what to say and decided against words. He closed the distance between them, slid a hand into her tangled hair and brought his lips to hers. She went taut for a split second before her body went pliant against his.

Hayden let loose the fierce desire inside, taking her mouth roughly. His hand laced into her hair and tugged, exposing her neck. Nipping at her earlobe, scraping his teeth down her neck, he could barely maintain his control. He stroked down her back, cupping her bottom and pulling her against his arousal—hot, hard and aching. The sound of her breathing drove him on. He tore at her clothes, as she did his. When they were bare, he pressed her against the door and plastered himself against her. Her soft curves gave against the hard planes of his body. He pulled back and just looked at her.

Her honeyed locks fell in a tangled mess around her face and shoulders. Her silvery eyes were dark with desire, her lips swollen from his kisses. Her full breasts rose and fell rapidly with her breath. He cupped her breasts in both hands. Her mouth was slightly parted, a whimper escaped when he thumbed her nipples. He leaned forward and drew one and then the other into his mouth. As she arched into his touch, he bit down sharply. The ragged cry that fell from her lips notched the lust pounding through him even higher. He leaned down, snatching a condom out of his jeans and rolling it on swiftly.

Hooking a hand under her thigh, he lifted it high and stepped into the cradle of her hips. Her breath came in pants, his heart battered against his ribs. He stroked into her folds, which were soaked. He groaned at the feel of her slick desire around his fingers when he delved inside.

"Hayden...I need..."

He couldn't get inside of her fast enough as her words rolled over him. He slipped his fingers out and nudged his cock into her entrance.

"Look at me."

His words were low and taut, his voice barely above a whisper. Her smoky eyes flew open, and he surged inside. Her hot, slick channel throbbed around him. He lifted her knee higher and thrust in to the hilt. Her eyelids fluttered, but she held his gaze as he began to stroke in and out of her. The feel of her around him wiped everything but sensation out of his mind. All he wanted was to drive her higher and higher, closer and closer to her release. The creamy clench of her channel pulsed around him as he pounded into her.

Only when her breath broke and she threw her head back with a cry, her body shuddering against his, did he let go. His orgasm crashed through him, the release of pressure so intense, only his grip on her held him up.

SHANA WAS SANDWICHED between the cold door against her back and Hayden's hot body. Pleasure pinged through her still, pulses of her orgasm shaking her. Hayden's head fell into her shoulder. His strong arms held her up. She breathed him in. She didn't want reality to intrude. She just wanted to be here, now, with him. After several long moments, he lifted his head, his warm caramel eyes meeting hers.

Twilight had fallen, and the light was faint. She could feel his heart beating against her skin. They were twined together. His eyes coasted over her face. He lifted a hand and brushed her hair away from her face, tucking a loose lock behind her ear. The small touch sent a soft shiver through her.

He cleared his throat. "Hey there," he said softly.

He said the perfect thing. Anything else and her mind would have twisted itself in knots over how to reply.

"Hey," she replied with a chuckle.

He slowly stepped back, easing her leg down as he did. She leaned against the door, thinking perhaps she should be embarrassed to have gone wild over him like that, but she didn't have it in her to care. He picked up her clothes and handed them to her before walking to the bathroom. She followed him and turned the shower on.

Without a word, she waved for him to join her. She wasn't ready to talk, but she wanted to be close to him. The steaming water soothed her. Hayden was quiet though his hands stayed on her as he soaped her and ran his hands through her hair when she returned the favor.

A while later, he lounged on a stool by the kitchen counter while she threw together an impromptu dinner of fettuccini with a light cream sauce and tomatoes. He'd just finished filling her in on his and Noah's interview with Theo.

"Wait, let me get this straight. Theo thinks your boss is running the smuggling network in Bozeman?" she asked, unable to hide the incredulity from her question.

He nodded. "Yup. I'm still trying to get that to sink in. I've known Clint for years. I can't say we're personally close, but I never suspected him. Never."

"How reliable do you guys think Theo is?"

He shrugged. "Thing is, there's no good reason for him to even have Clint's name. The fact that he does blows my mind."

"What now?"

"Jake's already doing his thing to look into Clint's online activities. Before we act on anything, I've still got a few other guys to interview. I've got a call into one of the detectives in Bozeman. They were cool having me come out here for this, but if we get anything actionable, they'll want to send their own guy."

Anxiety knotted in her chest. She'd been so relieved when Wallace had been arrested here, but she'd known it wasn't the end in the bigger scheme of things. When they'd gone out to Montana last winter, she realized the smuggling network extended far beyond Catamount. Hearing that Hayden's boss might be involved shouldn't have surprised her after everything, but it did.

She served the fettuccini on plates and slid one across the counter to him, tugging a stool to the opposite side to join him. Conversation moved onto lighter matters with Hayden asking casual questions about Catamount.

Hours later, Shana lay in bed beside Hayden and listened to the sound of his breathing. His body was a furnace, radiating heat. He slept on his side, his arm draped across her abdomen, his hand curled under a breast. She couldn't help it, but she savored the warmth and comfort of falling asleep with him. Her mind started riffling through worries. Should she be letting this happen with Hayden, what did it mean, what would she do if her heart wanted more than his...or if her heart wanted more than she was prepared to give?

If she stopped thinking and let her cat side through, she already knew how much she wanted from Hayden. But her human mind, so pushy sometimes, interjected, reminding her that her feelings for Hayden made her vulnerable—a dangerous place to go. Her mind kept flipping back and forth until Hayden shifted his weight, his hand sliding in a soft caress across the curve of her belly before he tugged her closer to him. She relaxed into his embrace, sleep finally stealing over her.

8

Shana gently pushed through the door into a patient's room. She had an early shift this morning. She'd expected to leave in the dark while Hayden was still sound asleep. He startled her by slipping out of bed while she was in the shower and starting coffee for her. She was a nurse at the hospital. Her work had gotten her through the last few years of her wasted marriage. Without that and her friends, she didn't know what she would have done over the last year. She loved her work because she liked helping and she loved interacting with patients. She worked on one of the general floors in the hospital, along with Phoebe.

The curtain was pulled around the patient's bed even though no one else was in other bed in the room. Shana walked quietly to the curtain and slowly slid it back. Gail Anderson was sound asleep. Gail was an old family friend and the police chief's wife. She'd been admitted to the hospital late last night after Hank brought her in reporting she'd fallen trying to get in the bathtub. Shana pulled Gail's chart and flipped through it. The x-rays done last night ruled out any broken bones, but her ankle was badly sprained. Glancing at her again, Shana carefully hung her chart up and turned to leave when she heard Gail say her name.

She turned back to find Gail trying to push herself up in bed. Shana stepped quickly to the side of the bed, adjusting the setting, so the bed slowly elevated.

"Hey Gail, no need to rush. The bed'll do all the work for you."

Gail's mouth tightened in a thin line. "I can sit up myself, you know."

Gail's hair, black with streaks of silver, was tied in a long braid. Her blue eyes were bright and snapping. Shana would have imagined Gail wouldn't have much patience with needing to rest, so she opted to avoid arguing the point.

"I'm sure you can, but why not take advantage of this snazzy bed? We just got these fancy new ones on this wing last month. Here's the remote." She proceeded to show Gail how to operate the remote control for her bed.

"How are you feeling this morning?" Shana asked once Gail had adjusted the bed to her liking.

Gail shrugged. "I'm fine. I can't believe Hank brought me here last night and that your brother admitted me for the night." Her eyes were accusing as she looked at Shana.

Dane was a doctor who had his own family practice, but he also covered emergency room duty at the hospital. Shana decided to stick with her plan not to argue any points with Gail. Gail had been born and raised in Catamount. She was a shifter and relentlessly practical and independent.

Shana demurred. "I'm sure Dane just wanted to make sure you stayed off your ankle long enough. Your chart indicates if your vitals are good today, you'll be discharged this afternoon. Mind if I check those?"

Gail harrumphed, but she easily offered her arm for a blood pressure check and tolerated the rest. Shana did as she did with most patients and let Gail lead the conversation. Which was fine until Gail brought up Callen. Shana had just about had enough of the comments on Callen and what he'd done. Gail's next comments startled her.

"I'm sure you're about to tune me out, but I didn't bring Callen up to blather on about how I can't believe what he did. I figured you might want to know not everyone thought you should have married him."

Shana swung to Gail, her eyes wide. "Huh? Gail, I don't know…"

Gail waved her hand dismissively. "You don't know why the hell I'm saying anything, right?" At Shana's nod, Gail continued. "Because he was never worth your time. That's why. It's not like I would have guessed Callen would get involved with drug smuggling, but it didn't surprise me when I found out. That whole Peyton family has always been a little too big for their britches. Knowing you the way I do, I'm guessing you feel terrible about what happened, but don't let Callen drag you down anymore."

Shana wasn't quite sure what to say, so she simply nodded.

Gail nodded firmly. "Right then." She

paused, her eyes softening. "I don't want to see you weighed down by his actions anymore than you already have been. That's all."

Shana took a breath. "I, uh…" She gathered herself. "I appreciate it, Gail. It's been a long year, to say the least."

Gail held her eyes for another moment before a sly smile stole over her face. "Don't suppose I can persuade you to let me out early today?"

Shana chuckled. "You're staying here until a doctor signs off on your discharge. Any other way and I'll be hearing about it."

HAYDEN TUCKED the phone against his shoulder. "I'm gonna need an extra week out here. Will that be okay?"

He was on the phone with his boss, Clint Reynolds. As much as he wanted to directly ask Clint how the hell his name ended up on the radar out here, Hayden didn't say a word.

"Do what you gotta do," Clint replied. "One of the detectives out here wants a call from you when you have any updates. I'll email his info to you in a few minutes."

"I'll keep an eye out for it." After a few

more minutes of discussion about projects he'd left behind, Hayden ended the call. He tossed the phone on the counter in Shana's kitchen and turned to look outside. Shana had left for work early, so he'd hopped on his laptop and plowed through his own work for most of the morning. He didn't bother to tell Clint he needed the extra time partly because he wanted as much time as he could have with Shana. Hayden also wanted enough time and distance from Clint to hopefully get some answers about his involvement in the smuggling network before Hayden returned to Montana.

He stood and strode over to the spiral staircase, walking upstairs to the small sitting area. The space up here offered an open view into a field with the forest and rolling mountains beyond it. Catamount lay at the edges of a beautiful wilderness. Hayden was staring out when there was a sharp knock at the door before Dane stepped through. He glanced up when Hayden said his name.

"Hey man. Thought I'd see if you want to ride into town with me to stop by Jake's office. Knowing him, he was probably up all night chasing down leads on your boss."

Hayden made his way back downstairs.

"Sure. I finished up most of my work for now." He walked to the counter, closed his laptop and strode to the room across the hall from Shana's. Conveniently, he'd left his bag in there. He wasn't up for any awkward moments with Dane just yet.

He grabbed his jacket and followed Dane out to his truck. A short drive later, they walked into Jake's office. Jake, as Hayden was coming to discover, had a laser focus. His eyes were glued to his computer screen when they entered. He didn't look up or greet them. Dane snagged one of the chairs by Jake's desk, gesturing for Hayden to take another. After a few moments of quiet, Jake swiveled away from his computer and ran a hand through his hair.

"Well, if you couldn't believe your boss was involved, you might want to get ready to accept it. Thing is, I saw his emails before but they're all aliases, so I didn't have a source to track them back to. Once you got Clint's name from Theo, I was able to dig deeper and trace the aliases back to him. He's in deep. His tracks go back over three years. It's like a spider web once I get back that far, one connection after another. Your boss has been conveniently using his position as cover. You might have been busy working on this, but he's been blowing off law enforcement requests for support left and right. He says yes just enough to keep them from getting suspicious. There are enough shifters and people involved out there that bringing him in will be a big help, but there'll be plenty of work left after that. You were right Montana isn't the center of all this though. From what I can piece together, the bright idea for using shifters to transport started somewhere in Colorado. Clint's given them a lot of cover in Montana and elsewhere out West though, so if your local guys can slap him with some charges, that should shake things up a bit."

Jake leaned back in his chair with a sigh, his gaze bouncing between Hayden and Dane. He appeared to be considering his thoughts. "You said one of the detectives out there would want updates?"

Hayden nodded. "Yeah. I spoke to Clint this morning about my time out here. He mentioned he'd be emailing me with the detective's info. I'm guessing it's one of the guys I've dealt with before. I hate saying this, but maybe you should do a little online digging on him before we assume he's not involved. All along, Clint directs the action on stuff like this. Not just with the smuggling network. If our office gets a request for back up from law enforcement on land management issues, hunting or whatever, it goes to him and he funnels it to me or someone else. From the start, he gives me the point person's name in any situation. For all I know, he's got help making sure investigations don't get too far."

"I'm with you there. You've got time and distance. Let's use it," Dane said.

Jake nodded. "I'm on it. Just get me the name of the detective."

Hayden dug his phone out of his pocket and pulled up his email. As promised, Clint had already emailed him the info. Hayden quickly forwarded the email to Jake. "Should show up in your email any second now." He leaned back in his chair, drumming his fingers on the armrest. "This is a clusterfuck. I can't believe Clint's been stringing us along for three years on this. He's even been there at a few of the arrests for some of the local dealers. Damn."

Dane's smile was bitter. "Trust me when I say we get the feeling. When Callen died, we had no idea what he'd been up to. The Peyton's are old school shifters—their family's been around for centuries. Those of us really close to what happened can hardly wrap our brains around it. Shifters have been mostly safe here for a long time because we don't advertise our existence. The people in Catamount who don't even know we exist only know a rich logging family got drawn into a smuggling scandal. They have no idea there's another layer that involved betraying half the town here and putting all shifters at risk. I'm guessing shifters in your area are gonna feel as furious as we do."

Jake had already tuned them out and was clicking away on his computer. Hayden nodded at Dane. "It's a little different there because Bozeman and the towns around where shifters live aren't quite like Catamount. You might not know it since you grew up here, but Catamount's legendary among shifters. It's where it all started. Shifters know each other out West, but we're more spread out. We don't have a history to protect. But it's not like we don't face the same dangers you do. Working for Fish & Wildlife gives me a pretty good idea what might happen if the existence of shifters became common knowledge. We'd be managed in some way. The shifters out there who've heard about the smuggling network are scared those guys are putting us in a risky situation. It'd be bad enough for people to find out shifters have been living amongst them for centuries, but way worse if they find out because shifters have been heavily involved in the drug trade."

Dane shook his head sadly. "Right. Once we get a little more info, if you want some of us to come out there to help you, we'd be happy to."

"Don't know if it's needed, but I appreciate the offer. Let's see what Jake finds out about the detective and go from there."

9

———

few days later, Shana sat at Phoebe's kitchen table idly tracing the grain of the wood in the table's surface. She'd stopped by after they'd shared a long shift at the hospital. The last few nights had been a blur of Hayden—hot, heavy nights that left her scrambling to regain control inside. When she was with him, her mind went black and primal desire took over. The idea that he could be near and they wouldn't become tangled up, skin to skin and almost breathing as one was inconceivable. She'd wanted to feel again after her heart and body felt so frozen, but she'd been entirely unprepared for the depth of feeling Hayden elicited. Phoebe was the friend she turned to when she needed advice. She was so lost, she wasn't even sure what might help.

The teapot whistled and Phoebe turned away from the sink to switch off the burner. In moments, she slid a hot cup of tea across the table to Shana and leaned back in her chair with a sigh.

"Damn, today was relentless. Is it just me or is the hospital busier than it ever was?" Phoebe asked.

Shana savored a swallow of hot tea and met Phoebe's eyes. "They keep saying Catamount's getting too big for the hospital. If you ask me, we can hardly keep up."

Her body ached in more ways than one. Hayden took her to places she'd never fathomed, often leaving her limp and sore the following morning. That combined with a day like today where she'd been on her feet and on the move for twelve hours straight left her exhausted.

"Moving on, what's up with you? You didn't say why you wanted to come over tonight, but I've known you long enough to know when you've got something on your mind."

Shana smiled ruefully. "So true. Just like I knew you had a thing for Jake for years even though you never said anything, I should've known you'd know something was up." She paused and took a breath. "This thing with Hayden is...kind of intense. I was married, so you'd think I had some experience with this, but it was never like this with Callen."

Shana ran out of words because she didn't know how to explain to Phoebe that her simple wish to act on the electricity that buzzed to life between her and Hayden had turned into something so much more. She hadn't expected to feel so emotionally intimate with him, connected on a level beyond words. By the time she came to terms with the state of her marriage and accepted it likely wouldn't get better, she'd only wished to find a way to stitch together the tattered remnants of her self-esteem and ask for a divorce. On the other side of that was the seemingly glorious temptation of being on her own again. She'd intended to be single forever. Perhaps a silly dream, but it seemed so freeing.

Then, Callen died and so many other concerns came to the fore that she couldn't focus on herself. All she could do was put one foot in front of the other and keep moving forward. She'd thrown herself into helping with the investigation into the smuggling network. That had offered her respite from her mind's hamster wheel of recriminations and regret. She recalled trying to consider how to process her grief over Callen when everything around him was emotionally muddied—the sad state of their marriage, his affairs, his betrayal of the shifter community, her own complicated feelings about why she'd married him to begin with, why she'd stayed as long as she had, and why she hadn't chosen to reach out to friends to talk about what was really happening.

Shana took a gulp of tea, savoring the heat, and glanced across the table at Phoebe. Phoebe was good at waiting and stayed quiet while Shana's mind did gymnastics. The part she shied away from was the hope that kept tapping its feet in her heart—hope that perhaps she might have stumbled into something special with Hayden. And hope was dangerous. She'd thought Hayden offered a simple escape—a fling with an out-of-town shifter. The threads between them were stitching tighter every day and nothing seemed simple. Now, the potential complications yawned before her—he lived halfway across the country and the mere thought of him not being near sent her heart into her throat. Though he hinted at his own feelings, she didn't know what they were and didn't have the courage just yet to ask.

When she looked up again, Phoebe was staring out the window. Shana followed her gaze. The kitchen looked out over a small field with a stream winding through it. The snow had mostly melted, lingering only in the shady areas near the trees. A blue jay squawked and flashed across the view, another right behind it. The two birds looped around, their blue wings catching the fading light, before they flew in unison to land on a bird feeder by the back deck. The feeder swung under the force of their landing.

Phoebe's voice startled her after the several moments of quiet. "It sounds like Hayden might be more than you bargained for."

Shana swung her gaze away from the window to find Phoebe's warm, dark brown eyes on her. She nodded. "And here I couldn't figure out how to explain it," she commented with a wry smile.

Phoebe chuckled softly before her expression sobered. "I can't tell you what you should do. Unfortunately, I don't know

Hayden like you knew Jake when I was half out of mind over what to do about him. But, I do know it generally doesn't help to keep your feelings hidden. Let him know what going on. You might find that helps clear up your own feelings."

"Easier said than done." Shana swallowed against the tightness in her throat. She wasn't ready to dive into interpreting her feelings. The moments when she managed to shut her brain up, she knew what she felt with Hayden was right and true. What she didn't know was what to do about it and where it would lead.

"Of course it's easier said than done. I know how hard it is. I spent a few too many years avoiding my feelings for Jake. Fortunately, we found our way through it, but don't think for second I don't regret how much time we wasted. Just don't let a good thing pass you by because you're afraid to say out loud what you're experiencing. I'm not saying that will help you decide what to do, but hiding your feelings sure as hell won't."

The tightness eased only slightly in her throat when Shana took a deep breath. She held Phoebe's eyes and nodded. "Right. I keep telling myself somehow I'll reach a point where I can feel settled inside, but the last few years keep throwing curveballs my way." She didn't say aloud that the few times she truly felt peaceful inside were when she was twined close to Hayden after they'd temporarily burned the fire between them down to embers. Then, only then, did she feel peaceful, the warm buzz of connection with him anchoring her inside.

HAYDEN GLANCED around Roxanne's Country Store and couldn't help but smile. This place was hopping every time he'd been in here, which turned out to be almost every day. Today, he was meeting Noah here before they headed back to the county jail for a few more interviews. The local detective from Montana, Glen Bowen, would be joining them there. Jake hadn't been able to find anything damning about Glen that would link him to the smuggling network, so they'd decided to move ahead and loop him into what they heard about Clint.

In the short time Hayden had been in Catamount, he'd grown to appreciate Noah's quiet, steady presence. Noah kept a low profile, but Hayden sensed he generally knew far more about what was going on than he shared. He tended to hang back, watch and wait. Hayden figured he was ideal to join him when they first met with Glen. Hayden had worked with Glen in a professional capacity on many occasions, but he thought Noah would sense if there was any reason for suspicion with Glen. The line at the counter opened up in front of him, and Hayden looked up to find Roxanne smiling at him.

"Hey Hayden! I'm gettin' pretty used to seeing your face around here. I might miss you when you go back to Montana," Roxanne offered with a grin.

"I can't seem to stay away from here. I know I'll miss seeing you every day, along with your coffee." He glanced around. "Seems like just about everyone in town comes here. Can't say there's a place quite like this in Montana." As the words left his mouth, Shana danced through his thoughts. She was the source of his draw to Catamount, but places like Roxanne's added to its charm.

"I'd like to take all the credit, but my grandfather got this place hoppin' long before I inherited it." Roxanne's eyes traveled past him, her smile widening again.

He turned to see Noah walking up behind him.

Roxanne teased with Noah for a moment before catching Hayden's eyes again. "What'll it be for you today?"

Hayden quickly ordered a coffee and a breakfast sandwich before stepping aside to wait while Noah ordered. They headed outside with their food to go and climbed into Noah's truck. Even though Hayden offered to drive, Noah shrugged it off. After another scenic drive and a few hours of interviews later, they walked outside with Glen Bowen. Glen leaned against his rental car, hands tucked in his pockets, and glanced between Hayden and Noah.

Glen was tall, lanky and weathered with gray hair and bright blue eyes. He loved the wilderness of Montana and was a dogged detective. He was a shifter and happened to be one of the few in law enforcement in their area in Montana, unlike in Catamount where it appeared almost everyone on the police force was a shifter. Glen ran a hand through his hair and sighed. "Figure now's as good a time as any to let you know I've had a bead on Clint for about a year now. I can't tell you how relieved I was when you told me his name came up in one of your interviews with the guys out here."

Hayden held Glen's gaze for a long moment. He shook his head. "Why didn't you say something before?"

Glen kicked his boot against the tire. "Same damn reason you probably thought twice about talking to me and then some. Clint's your boss and has been for years. For all I knew, you were involved too. When I say I had a bead on him, it's not like I had anything other than a few unsubstantiated rumors. My guess was if Clint was involved, he wasn't getting his hands dirty. After today, it's safe to say that's the case except for the money trail."

Fury rose in Hayden, but he batted it away. Clint was thousands of miles away. Getting worked up over his manipulations wouldn't do a bit of good now. He shook his head and met Glen's eyes. "I get it. I'd have wondered about me too. What do we do now?"

Noah glanced around the parking lot and gestured to them. "Let's have this conversation somewhere other than here. You planning to head to Catamount?" He directed his question to Glen.

At Glen's nod, Noah pulled his keys out. "Follow us then. We'll meet at Jake's office and talk."

Hours later, Hayden drove home through the twilight mulling over what they'd learned today. The only person involved in Catamount who refused to work with them and consider a plea deal was Wallace Peyton. Everyone else wanted leverage however they could get it. Between their discussions and Jake's legwork, more pieces of the puzzle had fallen into place. In sum, Clint used his position to create some cover for the smuggling network in and around Bozeman. When law enforcement requested support checking on suspicious activity in remote areas, Clint only occasionally obliged. At first, the investigators didn't think much of it because they had plenty of cases to focus on and trying to corral a smuggling network was considered a long-term job. However, last year, Glen heard a few rumors about Clint, so they started doing their own follow up when Clint didn't offer help. In the end, they'd managed to shut down a few delivery and storage locations. Clint had tried to keep his hands from getting dirty, but he'd done enough to get in the money, which meant he'd allowed the network to use his family's hunting property outside of Bozeman and served as a main point of contact for the network from out-of-state. According to two of the guys they spoke with today, he also funneled shifters willing to smuggle into the network.

Hayden was still slightly stunned to realize Clint had been doing this right under his nose. He thought back to the first time he'd been asked to help law enforcement and check on a report about unauthorized use on federal lands. Clint had climbed on a soapbox and spewed nonsense about how he couldn't believe the young shifters would fall for the easy money. When Hayden reconsidered many of Clint's statements though, ones that stood out were his repeated comments about how they'd likely never get a handle on this because drugs would always be sold and smuggled. He took the position that the best they could do was peck away at the small fry.

Hayden came to a stop in the circular driveway in front of the guesthouse. As soon as he pulled up, his mind shifted gears, thoughts of Shana racing to the fore of his consciousness. Every night he spent with her only deepened his feelings. Shana was like no other woman. She called to him on every level of his being—human and lion, mental, emotional, and physical. He sensed she had reservations about them and kept turning over in his mind how to convince her she needn't worry. He knew beyond any doubt she was meant to be his. He'd already considered and reconsidered what to do about the potential geographic challenges. He'd decided he'd return to Montana after this and hopefully be able to close the door on the smuggling network before returning to Catamount. There wasn't enough tying him to Montana to keep him there. Shana alone was enough reason to relocate to Catamount, but there were plenty of other benefits. He'd already put a few feelers out on whether he could transfer to a position in this area and found some promising options.

He stepped out of the truck, his body humming with anticipation when he walked through the door to be greeted by the view of Shana's delectable bottom as she leaned over to look for something in one of the kitchen cabinets.

10

———————

Shana pulled a baking tray out of the cabinet and moved to stand up, only to come to a quick stop when she felt a sharp tug on her hair and noticed several loose strands of her hair caught in the hinge on the door. She set the tray down and carefully untangled her hair, jumping at the sound of Hayden's voice.

"Stay right there as long as you want." His words slid over her, warm and smooth. She could hear the smile in his voice.

She couldn't help the giggle that escaped. Hayden had that effect on her. After years of heaviness in her heart, he elicited a light, frothy feeling inside. Even with her mental machinations over him, when he was near she forgot all of that. With a smile, she freed the last strand of hair from the cabinet hinge and picked up the tray again. Hayden's warm, strong palms curled around her hips and stroked down around her bottom as she stood. His touch instantly sent her pulse skittering wild and flutters twirling through her belly. By the time she set the tray on the counter and turned, her breath was short, her body was suffused with heat, and she was slick with desire.

His warm caramel eyes met hers, teasing and dark. Without a word, he brought her flush against him and fit his mouth over hers. His tongue swept in her mouth and his hands cupped her bottom, firmly pulling her against his arousal. He felt so good—so, so good. She'd come to crave the delicious quiver he sent racing through her veins. Hot, liquid need pulsed through her with every beat of her heart. He gentled his kiss, slowly pulling back. His breath came in short pants. She was dazed, barely able to think. All she wanted was to tear his clothes off and have him. Inside of her. Now.

"Hey there," he said softly.

He slid one of his hands slowly away

from its grip on her bottom, stroking up her side, curling over a breast and thumbing a nipple before lifting it to trace her lips. She couldn't resist flicking her tongue out and drawing the tip of his finger into her mouth. His eyes darkened when she swirled her tongue around before releasing it.

"Hey," she finally replied. "How was your day?"

His eyes sobered. "Hard to say. Productive, but depressing. Yours?"

Worry flickered in her mind. She knew he'd gone back to the county jail with Noah today to meet up with the detective from Montana.

"Mine was busy. But I only worked a shift and a half today, so I'm not dead on my feet, just pretty damn tired."

Hayden's fingers circled her lips once more before moving to sift through her hair. Soft shivers raced through her. Every touch fed into the fire between them. She tilted her eyes up to his. "I was about to start something for dinner."

He grinned, but didn't step back. The heat of his shaft rested against her belly, hard and pulsing. "We could eat later." His grin widened when he trailed his fingers down the side of her neck. She shuddered, taut with need. He traced a sizzling path down between her breasts and began methodically unbuttoning her shirt. By the time her shirt fell open, she was on fire, need coursing through her. She yanked at his clothing. His shirt joined hers on the floor while she tore his jeans open. She hummed her pleasure at the feel of his velvety hard cock in her hand.

She shoved him back against the counter and knelt down. She pushed his jeans down around his hips and stroked her tongue along the underside of his cock. His breath came out in a long groan and his hand laced in her hair. She took her time, licking, stroking, and sucking, savoring the salty tang of his pre-cum. His body was taut, his thighs rock-hard under the slide of her palms. In a swift move, he tugged on her hair.

"I need to be inside of you," he bit out.

She gave him one last stroke, drawing him all the way into her mouth, the head of his cock bumping against her throat before standing. His gaze burned into her, notching the heat higher inside. Her sex clenched, drenched with need. He shoved at her jeans, yanking them down. She kicked them free.

He fumbled in his pocket and swore, his eyes slamming up to hers.

"Forgot to pick up condoms today."

He didn't pause and slowly curled his hands around her hips and lifted her to the counter. *"Have to do this."* His palms slid up her calves and thighs, the calloused surface sending slivers of fire through her. He pushed her thighs apart and looked up as he stroked a finger into her folds, dripping with desire. Her breath came out on a groan as he slid one finger and then another into her channel. She forced herself to focus and held his eyes. "I'm on the pill, you know. Until you, there was no one for three years."

As she spoke, she wondered if she was half out of her mind, but she trusted him completely. She wasn't worried about protection. The tiny corner of her that worried she was in too deep tried to speak up, to say it wouldn't be smart to let herself feel him the way she wanted. But that voice couldn't be heard over the din of need crashing through her, the primal instinct driving her to get as close as possible to Hayden.

He held her gaze for an electric moment before nodding once sharply. Then, he circled his thumb around her clit as he pumped his fingers in and out of her channel. Her breath came out on a sob as pressure tightened inside of her. His eyes fell from hers when he leaned forward to bring his mouth against her. She spiraled into a place of need and sensation, everything narrowing to the feel of his fingers inside her throbbing channel and his tongue stroking around and through her folds. On her gasp, he drew her clit into his mouth sending her tumbling over the edge. Her orgasm ripped through her, pleasure streaking outward from her core in waves. By the time he drew away, she could barely move.

He dragged his fingers up, leaving a wet trail of her desire over her belly and circling her nipples. He nudged her chin up with his knuckles and brought his mouth to hers in a breath-stealing kiss. Just when she couldn't have imagined wanting more, he started the process all over. Hot, wet, drugging kisses. His lips, teeth, and tongue wreaking havoc on every inch they covered. The feel of his cock nestled against her slick folds. When she begged, he dragged the head of his cock back and forth until she was writhing against him, desperate to feel him inside of her. In a swift surge, he sank into her. He curled his hands on her hips and dragged her to the edge of the counter.

The feel of him filling her and stretching her pushed Shana closer and closer to the brink. He held her roughly as he pounded into her. She curled her legs around his hips, frantic to have him closer and deeper, savoring the scrape of his stubble on her neck, the bite of his teeth on her nipple. The coil of need tightened with each stroke. A quick flick of his thumb where their bodies joined as he thrust deeply inside, and she toppled over, pleasure ricocheting through her. As her channel clenched his length, he ached back on a cry, pulsing into her. He dipped his head forward on a breath, his forehead coming to rest against hers.

Several long moments later, Hayden lifted his head slowly. Shana opened her eyes to find his on her. Without a word, he leaned forward and took her lips in a leisurely kiss. He adjusted his grip on her hips and lifted her against him. Without releasing his grip, he shouldered his way through her bedroom into the bathroom. She rested her head against his shoulder, secure in his hold. He eased her down once they were in the shower and steaming hot water cascaded around them.

THE FOLLOWING AFTERNOON, Shana headed home, planning first to stop by Dane's house to drop off seedlings for Chloe's greenhouse. A co-worker at the hospital tended to go overboard when it was time to prep for gardening and always had more than she needed. Her phone rang as she wound along the road toward home. She tapped the screen on her dash to answer.

"Oh thank god you answered!"

Phoebe's greeting startled her. "Could we start with hello?" Shana countered.

"Fine, hello. I'm calling to tell you Dane knows about you and Hayden. I thought you'd want a heads up before you see him."

"What?!"

Shana didn't want to care what Dane thought of her relationships, but he'd been overprotective and worried about any woman he cared about ever since Callen died and two of Callen's associates from the smuggling network kidnapped Chloe. Shana also hadn't the heart to talk with him about the true state of her marriage to Callen before he died, so she didn't know how he'd react to learning she was involved with anyone. He'd probably be pissed Hayden hadn't told him. Which infuriated her. Dane would think he had a right to be her gatekeeper when he didn't.

"Jake says Dane stopped by the guesthouse last night and saw you two kissing through the window," Phoebe explained.

"Great, just great. I'm on my way to his house right now. I promised Chloe I'd drop off the seedlings from Helen at work."

Phoebe's sigh was audible through the car speakers. "If I were you, I'd just go talk to him. It's not like he gets to have an opinion about your personal life, but you know he'll have one. Jake usually isn't an ass, but he was all brother-in-charge when it came to Lily. He had enough sense to listen when I told him he needed to back off, but still."

"Dammit. This is not what I wanted to deal with today."

"If it's any consolation, Jake says Dane respects Hayden."

"I'm not sure if that's a good thing or not. He probably expected Hayden to ask for permission or some bullshit like that."

Phoebe chuckled. "Right. Well, I didn't want you to bump into him without knowing."

"I know. Thanks for calling. I'll let you know how it goes."

Her stomach knotted as she turned into the driveway that wound past the guesthouse where she was staying and ended at the colonial farmhouse Dane shared with Chloe. Trying to come to terms with her feelings about Hayden was complicated enough without her brother inserting his opinion into the situation. Shana parked quickly and grabbed the two trays of seedlings, stacked atop each other inside lidded boxes, and carried them to the front door. When she climbed up the steps, the front door swung open. Chloe stood there smiling.

"Hey! I heard you pull up. Let me get those." Chloe reached for the two trays and carefully shifted their weight into her hands. Her honey blonde hair was tied in a ponytail. Her green eyes were bright as she glanced over her shoulder and nudged her head, indicating Shana should follow her. They walked through the formal entryway and living room before moving down a short hallway into the kitchen at the back of the house. Chloe set the seedling trays on the kitchen counter and lifted the lids to examine them.

"This is perfect! She's got tomatoes, herbs and more in here." Chloe glanced up at Shana. "Thank you so much for bringing these for me. I can't wait to get a garden going this summer!"

Shana shrugged. "No problem. Helen goes a little crazy with gardening every year, so now she knows you're into it, she'll send more your way. If you want to stop by the hospital one of these days, I can introduce you to her."

"Awesome! Maybe I can swing by later this week." She spun away and gestured to the coffee pot. "Coffee?"

"Sure." Shana sat down on a stool by the counter. When Chloe slid a cup of coffee over to her, she caught her eyes. "Has Dane mentioned anything to you about me and Hayden?"

Chloe bit her lip and scrunched her nose. "Yeah. I was going to warn you he might say something to you about it."

Shana brushed her hair away from her face. "Phoebe called because I guess Dane mentioned it to Jake. Just tell me what he said."

Chloe sighed. "He said he stopped by last night on the way home and saw you two making out through the entry window. He was all huffy about it last night, but I reminded him you're thirty-one years old and way past the age where he has a say in what you do. I don't know if it helped much."

Shana took a sip of coffee and stared at the counter, tracing the edges of the tiles. "Dane wasn't horrible when we were younger, but it's not like he had much to get overprotective about. I didn't date too much in high school and started seeing Callen when I was a sophomore in college. We got married and that was it."

Chloe eyed her. "I hope it's okay I told him what you said about how bad things were with you and Callen at the end. He's been so worried about you since Callen died and how you were handling what Callen did, I thought it might help him understand better."

"You told him that last night?"

"No, before that. He said he was relieved to know. He's been so pissed off at Callen that I think he didn't know how to support you.

For some reason, it made him feel better to know things were already shitty with you and Callen before he died. I'm not sure if that makes sense..."

Shana interjected. "It does to me. I already knew Callen was an asshole before he died. I didn't realize how much of an asshole he was, but it wasn't like I had to learn the truth about him after we'd had this amazing marriage. That would have been even harder."

"I guess so," Chloe said softly. "So, are things with Hayden serious? You know Dane'll ask about that."

"It's none of his damn business," Shana said, anger and anxiety knotting together inside. It wasn't any of Dane's business, but it irked her he'd ask because she was betwixt and between. When her mind wasn't in the middle, everything made sense with Hayden. She'd fallen asleep last night with him spooned behind her, his hand resting on the curve of her abdomen, his lips soft on her neck, and she wanted nothing more than to stay right there with him...forever. When she'd gone about her day later, her mind did gymnastics over him—wondering how she could feel so right with him, wondering what to do about the hope that simmered in her heart, and wondering how to manage the geographic challenges if they were to try to make something real of the flame that burned so hard and bright between them. Most of all, she wondered how she could ever have what seemed possible with Hayden—a man she wanted with her whole heart and body who wanted her in return and who was good and true and everything the sham of her first marriage had taught her wasn't possible.

"I think he knows it's none of his business, but he doesn't really care."

Chloe's blunt assessment made Shana chuckle. "No, he wouldn't care if it's none of his business or not." She glanced at the clock on the wall. "Any idea when he'll be home? I'm figuring I'd rather just clear the air now."

"He should be home any minute. If you'd prefer if I get the hell out of the way, I can make myself busy out in the greenhouse," Chloe offered.

Shana shrugged. "Doesn't matter to me. Honestly, if you're here, Dane is less likely to be a complete ass about it."

As if they'd conjured Dane simply by speaking of him, the sound of the front door opening and closing could be heard in the distance followed by footsteps making their way to the kitchen. Dane turned the corner into the kitchen, his blue-gray eyes bouncing from Chloe to Shana. He quickly stepped to Chloe's side and dropped a kiss on her cheek before tossing his jacket on a chair by the table. Chloe made small talk even though the room had gone tense the moment Dane entered.

Shana finally had enough. "Okay, spit it out," she demanded, catching Dane's eyes when he leaned a hip against the counter with his arms crossed.

"What are you talking about?" The lines around his mouth were tight, and his expression was controlled.

Shana rolled her eyes. "Let's just say I received a warning you might have something to say about me and Hayden."

Dane glanced to Chloe who put her hands on her hips and glared at him. "I'm not the first one who said something to her, and even if I was, it shouldn't matter."

Dane took a deep breath, his eyes swinging back to Shana. "All I care about is making sure you don't get hurt again. Hayden seems like a nice guy, but..."

"But what?" Shana threw her hands up in the air.

Dane stared at her. "You've had a lot to deal with this year. Do you even know what you want? What Hayden wants? I'll tell you this: if all he wants is a fling, that's not cool with me. You don't need someone else to use you the way Callen did. All Callen wanted from you was your family connections. I didn't see it at first, but it became pretty clear over time. Maybe you don't want to talk about it, but Chloe told me how things were for you two before he died." He paused and took a deep breath, a flash of pain arcing through his eyes. "You didn't deserve any of that. Callen was a fuckin' loser on so many levels. I don't want to see you hurt again. Hayden seems like a good guy, but I wouldn't have guessed he'd have let this happen, so…"

Shana interrupted. "I started it, so don't go blaming him." Her face was flushed with anger and embarrassment. The last thing she wanted to do was fess up to her brother that she was the one who persuaded Hayden, not the other way around. But she didn't want him thinking otherwise.

Dane's eyes widened. He waited a beat. "Whether you started it or not doesn't change the fact that he knows what you've been through..."

Chloe cleared her throat. Dane started to speak again when Chloe put a hand on his arm. He forcefully snapped his mouth closed, his lips in a tight line.

Shana glared at him. "Whatever you think, lecturing me about it isn't going to change anything." She couldn't say why, but her brother's worry about her only fed into the cauldron of confusion swirling in her mind about Hayden. Dane wasn't spelling it out, but she could guess what prompted his concerns. She was too emotionally fragile, it was too soon, she didn't know what she wanted, what was she doing diving into a fling like this? On and on and on. The thought that swam under the surface all the time...

You weren't supposed to fall for him. You weren't supposed to want him to the core of your body, heart and soul. You can't pretend that's not happening. Because it is. Denying it won't help.

She batted her inner critic away and tried to quiet the hope that kept springing up inside like flowers poking through snow in the spring. She glanced between Dane and Chloe. Chloe's eyes were warm with concern.

Whatever Dane was feeling, he was doing a damn good job of keeping it to himself. She sensed anger girded by his concern for her. She met his eyes again. "I get you'd be worried, but let me figure it out. Okay?"

Dane nodded slowly. She gulped the last of her coffee and stood to leave.

11

Hayden sat at the kitchen table in the guesthouse, his laptop on the table, as he caught up on work emails. Shana had left for work early this morning. Hayden glanced up at the sound of a sharp knock at the door. Dane stepped inside.

"Hey man, how's it going?"

Dane nodded and walked to the table, tugging a chair out and sitting. Hayden clicked out of his email and closed his laptop. Dane was quieter than usual. When Hayden met his eyes again, he knew instantly that somehow Dane knew about him and Shana. His mind whirred over last night. Shana had come home irritable and out of sorts. When he'd asked how she was doing, she shrugged it off and dragged him to her. She'd proceeded to drive him near out of his mind, as she was wont to do any moment they were alone. Yet, she'd had a reckless edge to her last night. He didn't know what to do about the depth of intimacy he felt with her combined with the newness of their connection. He'd wanted to push, to ask what was on her mind, but he'd sensed she would only shut him down, so he left it alone. Looking at Dane, he wondered if Shana knew what Dane knew.

Hayden took a breath and contemplated his position. He remembered how he'd felt last winter when he met Shana. The spark of attraction burned bright the first time he laid eyes on her. At the time, he hadn't a clue of the circumstances around her marriage with Callen and had told himself she was off limits out of respect for what she was going through and his respect for Dane. The first day he saw her when he arrived in Catamount, those same thoughts spun through his mind. Then, she'd gone and kissed him, a kiss he hadn't hesitated to enjoy the moment her lips met his. Beyond that, she'd shared the truth about the years of her barren marriage and made it clear what she wanted. Even then, he'd thought he was taking a step into something far less than what he'd come to understand.

The word love pierced through his thoughts like a shot. It had danced along the edges of his consciousness ever since the day he'd seen her in lion form in the woods. His lion knew exactly what lay between them. His awareness that Shana needed to be ready on her own terms and he couldn't force it held him at bay. The other issue was purely logistical—how and when to relocate to Catamount. He hadn't broached that topic yet with Shana. He wasn't ready to put his heart on the line and scare her away. No matter how primal his feelings for her were, no matter the depth of power of the connection between them, he sensed Shana was still untangling her feelings. She was a strong woman and not to be pressured, so he didn't dare play his cards too soon. He pondered how to explain all of this to Dane.

Before he had a chance to say anything, Dane shifted. He stood before Hayden, his hackles raised and snarling. Hayden's instinct drove him to shift. Dane growled and lunged toward him. Hayden didn't want this and certainly not inside, so he backed away and pushed through the door, dashing into the yard and across the field toward the trees. Dane was right on his heels. Hayden clung to the threads of his human reason. He knew Dane needed this, so he'd find a way to balance that with keeping it from getting out of hand.

Hayden spun around once they were in the shelter of the forest. Dane bounded off of a tree and dodged past Hayden, swiping him as he passed. Hayden snarled and leapt onto a tree branch. Dane was lean and quick. He tracked Hayden's every move. They dashed through the trees, dodging and swiping. Hayden could feel Dane's anger burning in every move. Hayden lost focus for a split second when Shana crossed his thoughts. In mid-air, he slipped, losing his grip on a branch. Dane pounced, growling in his face. After a long moment, quiet fell and Dane slowly backed away.

A while later, Hayden slumped into a chair in the kitchen and eyed Dane cautiously. They'd quietly returned to the house and shifted back into human form.

Dane cleared his throat. When Hayden glanced up, Dane's eyes were hard. "Shana says it's none of my business, but I figure it is. She's my sister, and she's been through hell. I don't know what your intentions are, but if you hurt her, you'll answer to me," Dane said flatly.

Hayden leaned back in his chair and held Dane's gaze. "Fair enough."

Dane arched a brow. "What are your intentions? And don't you dare tell me it's none of my business. I trusted you. I'm doing my damnedest not to make this ugly, but you'd better be honest with me." Dane's voice was low and threaded with anger.

Hayden was relieved to simply get this conversation out of the way because he hadn't liked keeping this from Dane. The only reason he had was he felt like it was Shana's choice, not his. He held Dane's gaze. "I didn't plan it this way, but as far as I'm concerned, there's no one else for me. I know Shana's had a rough year and maybe the timing isn't ideal, but all I'm waiting for is for her to be ready. I've already decided I want to move to Catamount. I don't have any family left in Bozeman to keep me there, and I can't imagine Shana being anywhere other than Catamount. I like it here. It's pure logistics on that end. I just..." He paused, his throat tightening. He wanted to blast through the waiting and convince Shana what he knew to be true—that she was the only woman for him.

Dane's hard expression softened. He uncrossed his arms and eyed Hayden. "So that's how it is then?"

Hayden ran a hand through his hair. "That's how it is."

Dane was quiet for a moment, his eyes considering. "Shana doesn't do pressure well."

Hayden nodded, his chest and throat still tight with emotion. "I gathered. I'll wait. I haven't told her exactly how I feel yet."

Dane leaned forward, his elbows resting on the table. "Might help if she knew."

"You don't think she might feel pressured?"

Dane shrugged. "I think she pressures herself more than anyone else can. I figure it's best if she knows where you stand."

Hayden considered Dane's words. "Maybe." He took a breath, trying to ease the emotion clogging his throat. "Look, I respect you. I don't want you to think..."

Dane leaned back and waved a hand dismissively. "I was pissed, but I got it out of my system." He paused and chuckled. "Shana pretty much jumped down my throat about it and made it clear she's the one that started it. I'd still be pissed if I thought you might hurt her, but I'm not getting the sense I need to worry about that now. I reserve the right to get pissed in the future if anything changes though, so you'd better be good to her."

Hayden chuckled. "Right. You have my word."

Conversation moved on somehow. A while later after Dane left, Hayden sat upstairs in the small sitting area, staring out into the woods behind with the mountains rising beyond. The wheels in his mind turned as he considered when and how to tell Shana how much she meant to him.

12

———————

Shana returned home late after another double shift, her body tired and weary. When she went inside, she found Hayden had made dinner. She'd discovered he was a remarkably good cook. Tonight, he'd made a simple stew in the slow cooker, explaining he hadn't been sure what time she'd be home. After eating a quiet dinner and mellowed with wine, Shana had tumbled into sleep, his strong arms around her.

The next morning she woke to the sound of low male voices. She lay in bed, contemplating a brief conversation from last night when Hayden told her Dane had confronted him about her. She'd fessed up that Dane had confronted her about it the day before, but she hadn't had the energy to talk about it yet. Hayden had been gracious enough to say he understood, but he didn't offer anything else. She couldn't help but wonder. She didn't have to be in for work until this afternoon, so she tugged a robe on and headed for the door. She paused when she realized the other voice was Dane's.

"So, did you get up the nerve to tell Shana how you feel?" Dane's question was soft with a hint of teasing.

Her spine stiffened, annoyance flashing through her. She had to quell the urge to shove through the door and give them both a piece of her mind. She waited to hear Hayden's response.

"Not yet. Trying to find the right time." His noncommittal reply only inflamed her irritation.

"Well, don't waste too much time."

Shana shoved through the door, tightening the belt on her robe as she strode into the kitchen. They were seated together at the table. Hayden pushed his chair back and stood. "Hey there, we just finished some omelets, but I've been waiting for you to get up before I made yours."

She fought against the pull to him. She wanted to go to him, tug him close for a kiss and bury her head in his strong chest. He was like her personal tuning fork, her body flexing toward him whenever he was near. Her emotions ran deep and she didn't know how to manage them. Hearing that her own brother (who had no right to be interfering in her personal life!) apparently knew more about how Hayden felt about her infuriated and embarrassed her at once.

When her eyes met Hayden's, a flush raced through her, her face and body instantly hot. Her eyes bounced away from his to Dane's. "Maybe you two could update me on whatever it is you're talking about." Her voice sounded high and shrill to her own ears, but she didn't care. Anger pulsed through her in waves.

HAYDEN STOPPED mid-stride and turned to Shana. Her face was flushed, her eyes snapping. *Fuck. Talking to Dane before you talked to Shana...really bad plan.* Hayden tried to gather his thoughts and think of what to say. He wished like hell Dane wasn't here at the moment because he knew Dane's presence likely amplified Shana's anger. She was angry with him for not talking to her first and angry with Dane for butting into her life. Dane pushed his chair back from the table and stood.

"Don't get pissed at Hayden about this. I talked to him yesterday. Far as I'm concerned, he's..." Dane started to say.

"Since when is it up to you to screen anyone I'm involved with?" Shana didn't bother to give Dane a chance to reply, swinging to Hayden. "So you have enough decency to mention my brother confronted you about us, but you don't bother to tell me whatever the hell your feelings are?" Hayden opened his mouth to reply, but she waved him away. "You know what? If you think my fucking brother has more right to hear how you feel than I do, than I don't care to hear it."

Hayden took a step toward her, curling his hand around her arm. She flung his touch away. "Shana, please..."

"No!"

His heart thumped, dread coiled in his stomach. He wanted to grab her and yank her to him, but he knew he couldn't. Not now. Forcing this would only lead her to push him away. He let his hand fall, clenching and unclenching his fist to keep from grabbing her again. She whirled away, turning back before she pushed through the bedroom door. "When I come back out, I think it's best if you stay in the other apartment here. Dane can help make sure the heater's running."

The door to her bedroom slammed shut. He stood there, the silence reverberating in the room. He turned and caught Dane's eyes. Dane hitched his brows up and shrugged.

"Sorry, man. I shouldn't have said anything. Give her some time. I know you mean a lot to her."

Hayden tried to quell the pain tightening inside, but he couldn't. He feared he'd lost Shana over the stupidest thing—not having the nerve to just tell her how he felt. He didn't have it in him to talk anymore. He nodded sharply at Dane. "Mind giving us some privacy?"

Dane stood up so quickly, he almost knocked his chair over. "Catch you later," he said over his shoulder on the way out the door.

Hayden took a breath and walked to Shana's bedroom door.

"Shana? Please let me explain," he called through the door.

There was a long silence before he heard footsteps pounding across the floor and the door flew open. Shana's silver eyes were dark with anger and laced with pain. "I don't want you to explain. I am so tired of everyone thinking I'm too fragile to tell me what's going on. I need some space. Just leave me alone." She turned away and closed the door quietly. The sound of the lock echoed through the hallway.

Hayden wanted to stay and wait for her to come out, but he knew he needed to give her the space she asked for, so he quietly gathered his things out of the spare bedroom and moved them into the other apartment. He stood by the windows and stared into the backyard. He knew he had only himself to blame. Shana's life had been tossed asunder over the past year with little she could do to control it. The last thing he should have done was anything to add to the idea that others had a say in her life. Dane, well-meaning and overprotective brother that he was, shouldn't have been the first to know how much Shana meant to Hayden.

⁓

A FEW DAYS LATER, Shana pushed through the door of Roxanne's Country Store and stepped outside. It was a bright, spring day. She took a deep breath, gulping in the earthy scents of new growth. Her heart was heavy as she tried to come to terms with the fact Hayden was likely leaving Catamount without talking to her again. She hadn't been able to bear staying near him, so she'd begged Phoebe to let her crash there the last few nights. Phoebe had grudgingly agreed, but Shana knew Phoebe was holding back from pushing her too hard on what she thought. Until this morning when Phoebe asked how long she was going to be stubborn. Phoebe's question had helped her dredge up the nerve to try to talk to him this morning, only to find him gone from the guesthouse when she stopped by.

Desperate, she called Dane this morning who told her Hayden was flying out of Portland in a few hours. As she approached her car, wondering where he was, she heard footsteps behind her. Shana whirled around. Hayden took two more steps, coming to a stop just in front of her. His caramel eyes locked with hers, and he didn't look away. His hair was messy, as if he'd run a hand through it a few too many times. He wore faded jeans and a navy t-shirt, his muscled arms and chest stretching the fabric. Longing and lust struck deep inside. Her body hummed with want, the way it always did anytime he was near her.

He reached for her hands, his warm strong grip closing around hers. Her heart pounded and her throat tightened. She'd missed him so much the last few days. She had thought she needed space. Perhaps she still did, but all she knew was she couldn't think clearly.

"I screwed up, Shana. This whole thing with you hit me sideways and I wasn't prepared. I shouldn't have talked to Dane about how I felt before talking to you. I can't change it, but I'm more sorry than you know."

He searched her eyes and took a breath. "Look, you said we'd figure it out if there was more to this. I don't know about you, but there is for me. It's tearing me up to leave with things like this, so you have to know how I feel. I love you."

His words pierced through her. Hope twirled madly in her heart. He squeezed her hands, freeing one of his and sliding it up into her hair. The feel of his touch almost hurt—it was so good and she'd missed him so. He closed his eyes. His shoulders rose and fell on a deep breath. Feelings crashed through her, and she tried to gather herself. When he opened his eyes again, they held hers steadily.

His voice rasped when he spoke again. "I didn't want to pressure you, but I can't leave without you knowing exactly where I stand. Every part of me wants you like I've never wanted anyone before. I meant to tell you I already planned to move here once you were ready. The only thing holding me in Montana is finishing up this damn investigation. After that..."

His words trailed off. Emotion rose inside of her. Tears clogged her throat and stung her eyes. He lifted a hand and traced her lips. The air shimmered around them. She could hardly breathe. Hayden's caramel gaze seared into her. Her heart battered against her ribs. His words scored her heart. He said everything she wanted to hear, and it terrified her. His thumb traced her lips, heat curling through her. When he fit his mouth over hers, sensation rushed through her. His hand cupped the back of her head, his thumb stroking the soft skin under her ear. She strained to get closer, desperate to feel him. Only a few days away from him, and it was as if she was starved. His tongue traced her lips, sweeping inside when she gasped. Her car was behind her. He came flush against her body and took a step. She felt the cool metal of her car against her back.

Hayden's kisses had the ability to drive her wild, make her forget everything but the feel of his lips on hers. This one was no exception and was layered with the unfulfilled feelings she'd been trying to tamp down. She wanted to lose herself in him, yet he gentled his kiss and pulled back. She opened her eyes, emotion welling inside.

Hayden stood there with her, their breath rising and falling in unison. Distant sounds filtered into her awareness—voices from the far side of the town green, a crow squawking and sparrows chattering. Hayden's eyes met hers, his gaze a mix of longing and sadness.

He cleared his throat, his words coming

out gruff when he spoke. "Don't forget this. I love you, but I'll wait until you're ready."

He stepped away, his hands sliding from her body. She felt bereft, missing his touch immediately. She forced herself to speak. "I, uh..." The words wouldn't come. She was too muddled, too overwhelmed.

"It's okay. All you have to do is call me. I'll be there."

She watched him walk away. The tears burning her eyes finally rolled down her cheeks.

13

A few days later, Shana pushed through the door at Roxanne's Country Store. It was a rainy, cool spring morning. The rain was melting the lingering patches of snow, but the chill seeped through her. She made a beeline for the deli. It was mid-morning, so the place wasn't at its busiest. She waited by the counter, perusing the specials listed on the chalkboard. Roxanne came through the swinging door that led to the back. She grinned as soon as she saw Shana.

"Hey there! How's it going?"

Shana tried to smile, but it wobbled and wouldn't hold. She thought she had her feelings under wraps, but it seemed she could only keep it together when she was at work. There, she was so busy she barely had time to breathe, much less think about how much she missed Hayden.

Roxanne's smile dissolved into a look of concern. She glanced around the deli before turning to the young woman who was busy assembling sandwiches on the far side of the prep area behind the counter. "Keep an eye on the counter, Becky. Okay?"

Becky glanced up and nodded. Roxanne waved for Shana to follow her, hooking her hand through Shana's elbow once she came around to the back of the counter. Roxanne led her into the back, past the office and into the small sitting room in the private quarters of the old home. Roxanne all but ordered her to sit in one of the comfy chairs and raced back out front. She returned moments later with two cups of coffee and handed one to Shana.

With a flourish, she sat down in the chair angled toward Shana. "Okay, what the hell is going on with you? Phoebe said you've been working yourself to death the last few days. She didn't say much about you and Hayden, but I happened to see you crying when he walked away the other day. Spit it out."

Shana's throat was tight and her heart hurt. She took a gulp of coffee and stared at the swirl of rich, dark liquid in the mug. "I screwed up," she said softly.

After a long silence, Roxanne cleared her throat. Shana looked up to find Roxanne's warm blue eyes on hers. Roxanne circled her hand for Shana to continue.

Shana took another gulp of coffee. "So, Hayden and I kind of had a thing."

"Had? Or have?"

Shana flushed. "I guess we have a thing. You know how things were with Callen and me. I just wanted to feel something, anything. And Hayden, well..."

At her long pause, Roxanne interjected. "He's hot."

Shana couldn't help the giggle that escaped her. "Yup, he's hot. I thought we could maybe have a fling. No harm done. But it turned into a lot more than that. I got pissed off when Dane talked to Hayden about it, as if he has any right to interfere in my personal life. The last few days he was here, I didn't even talk to him. When you saw us, well, he was leaving. He came to tell me how he felt."

Another long pause. Roxanne cleared

her throat again. "Let's get to the point. How does he feel?"

Shana's words came out softly. It almost hurt to say them. Because she couldn't quite believe it. "He said he loves me."

Shana looked up to find Roxanne's eyes on her. "And how do you feel?"

"I... I love him. I think."

Roxanne took a sip of coffee and nodded slowly. "Okay. So what's the problem?"

Shana chewed on her lip and traced the edge of her coffee mug. "I don't know. I mean, look at what happened with Callen. My marriage was a pathetic waste and he turned out to be a colossal asshole. What if I just have incredibly bad judgment in men? I don't think I could take it if things fell apart with Hayden the way they did with Callen."

Roxanne shook her head. "Honey, none of us could have imagined Callen would turn out to be as much of an ass as he was. I get why it took you so long to tell us how things were with him, but don't go comparing other men to him. Look around you. You know plenty of good men who'd never treat a woman the way Callen treated you. I can't say I know Hayden too well, but he's nothing like Callen. Even before I knew Callen treated you like shit and got in with drug smugglers, I knew he was kind of a jerk. He was always a bit too arrogant for my taste. You're one of my best friends, so I wanted to support you. I didn't think it was worth pointing out he was a tad too interested in himself. But Hayden, he's nothing like that. I don't even think he realizes how damn hot he is. He ignores all the women who stare at him. According to Dane, Jake, and Noah, he's a good guy. You said so yourself after you came back from Montana last year. I get why you might be thinking the way you are, but don't go there. If you love him, do something about it."

"What if it's too soon?"

"Too soon? How do you mean?"

"Since Callen died, since my life got turned upside down by everything he did."

Roxanne practically glared at her. "Don't be ridiculous! Callen died last year, and you two were married in name only for the last few years before that. If that's what's holding you back, you're being stupid."

Roxanne was never one to shy away from being completely blunt. Shana flushed again and took another gulp of coffee to gather herself.

"Okay then. I guess I'm..." Her words trailed off as she tried to explain.

"Thinking way too hard about this," Roxanne offered. "Trust me, it never helps. What does your gut tell you?"

Shana walked outside a while later and breathed deep, savoring the fresh air. The rain had stopped. She pondered Roxanne's last question to her. Listening to her gut meant tuning in to both sides of herself—lion and human. Therein lay the answer, and she already knew it. She had to see Hayden. As soon as possible.

14

Hayden kept himself busy at work since he'd been home. The reason was two-fold. He needed something to keep his mind off of Shana because thinking about her was painful. He'd promised himself he would give her the space and time to come to him on her own terms. The wait was excruciating. He had to wait though. Shana wasn't just any woman. She was destined to be his mate. To honor all that she was—strong, intelligent, and so sexy she brought him to his knees—he needed her to come to him freely.

Keeping busy at work also helped him manage the impulse to grab Clint, shove him against the wall and demand an explanation for the bullshit manipulation he'd been pulling off for the last three years. He absolutely could not do that. They'd developed a plan back in Catamount. Glen, the local detective here, was coordinating with local law enforcement to execute a series of arrests all at once for a number of the lower level players involved in the smuggling network. Hayden's role was mainly to track Clint's whereabouts the day of the arrests. The work the detectives had done before indicated Clint did clean up after the fact at any storage and delivery sites.

Hayden could handle the waiting, but it was hard when Clint dropped bullshit comments about the smuggling network and how frustrated he was with its annoying presence and tendency to pop up again and again. Hayden had enough sense to know, just as they did in Catamount, that knocking a few of the main players out wouldn't make the network disappear permanently, but they hoped to hobble it and make it harder for the network to regroup.

Early one morning, he received the call from Glen that the wheels were in motion. Hayden buried himself in reports to stay busy. Clint leaned through his door not long after he showed up at the office.

"I'm headed out to check on a complaint from one of the ranches on the western side of town. I'll..."

Clint was interrupted when the office door opened. He swung away from Hayden. Hayden stood and looked out into the reception area. His heart flew to his throat when Shana came through the entrance. She froze when she saw him. His heart slammed against his ribs. The effect she had on him was a powerful mix of emotion and pure physical need.

Clint looked at Shana. "Can I help you?"

Shana cleared her throat. "I was hoping to meet with Hayden."

Clint glanced from Shana into Hayden's office. "You have time for a meeting?" he asked. Clint appeared distracted, which was convenient because he didn't seem to be catching onto the tension emanating from Hayden to Shana. It was all Hayden could do not to walk to her, lift her in his arms and pour his feelings into a kiss. He shackled his urges, keeping his expression bland, and nodded at Clint. "Sure. Come on in," he replied, gesturing to Shana.

She walked toward him, her tawny hair loose around her shoulders. She entered his office and gently closed the door behind her. Without a word, she stepped in front of him, stopping mere inches away. The ache to touch her was so intense, he could barely contain it.

Her eyes, silvery and smoky, met his. "Hey," she said softly.

"Hey." His pulse pounded, longing washing through him in waves.

Before he could say another word, he heard the door in the reception area bang against the wall. Fear joined the collision of feelings inside of him. What he wanted to do was take Shana in his arms and carry her away. But he couldn't. Not now. Her eyes bounced from him to the door.

"Is everything okay?" she asked, her voice low.

He shrugged. "Let me see what's going on, okay?"

At her quick nod, he stepped around her and opened his office door. A man Hayden had never seen stood in the waiting room. He knew instantly the man was a shifter—the man felt as if he was about to shift right now. Energy pulsed from him.

Clint glanced in Hayden's direction before turning back to the man. "Why don't you come into my office? We can talk there," he said, his voice low and soothing.

The man shrugged and followed Clint into his office. Hayden turned back to Shana. He moved away from the door again, speaking barely above a whisper.

"You have no idea how much I want to get out of here and be anywhere alone with you. But no, everything is not okay. The police are in the middle of an arrest sweep. My job is to follow my boss wherever he goes without him noticing. I'm not sure who just showed up to see him, but I have a bad feeling."

He curled his hands around her arms and tugged her close because he couldn't resist having at least that for the moment. She pulled back and stroked her hand down his cheek. "I missed you," she whispered.

He took her mouth in a bruising kiss, frantic to soak up all he could as fast as he could. At the sound of raised voices coming from Clint's office, he pulled away. Shana's eyes were clear and concerned.

"Don't worry about me. I know you have to do this now. What can I do to help?"

"Shana, I know you can take care of your-self, but I don't want you anywhere near this. I'll give you my address. You can go there and wait." He snagged his keys off the desk and placed them in her palm.

He started to give her the address when the door to Clint's office flung open. The man who'd stopped by shifted and turned to face Clint again. With a roar, he swiped at Clint who shifted in response. When the unknown shifter turned away, his golden eyes coasted over Shana and Hayden standing by his of-fice door. When he postured and moved in their direction, Hayden couldn't hold back his lion. The moment the two men had shifted, his lion rumbled under his skin, calling to be set loose. He walked into the waiting area, his hackles raised and fury sim-mering. Shana glanced among them. In a flash, she shifted as well, swiftly moving to Hayden's side. The unknown shifter growled at Hayden and swiped in his direction. Shana streaked between them with a snarl, catching the other shifter on the throat.

Time blurred as events unfolded rapidly. Clint and his associate dashed through the windows at the back of the office with Hayden and Shana following. Hayden's human mind stayed engaged when he was in lion form, and he couldn't hold back the wry thought that the office windows had seen more than their fair share of breakage ever since the smuggling network had sprung up. Bitterly, he considered what he now knew— those shifters who seemed to randomly show up at the office were likely anything but random given Clint's role in the network.

Hayden silently called to Shana, pleading with her to stay back. He knew she understood, but she ignored him. She was glorious in lion form. Her movement was sleek and sinuous. She tracked the two lions with ease. They threaded into the foothills. Hayden knew the local police had sentries set up all over the area. Otherwise, he'd have hesitated to follow.

Clint and the other lion barreled through the trees until they reached a clearing where a cluster of hunting cabins was dispersed in the nearby area. Hayden had been out here before and warned away shifters after reports of trespassing and hunting out of season. Clint came to a stop and waited. Hayden wondered if Clint planned to try to maintain his cover or not. As soon as Hayden reached his side, he had his answer. Clint snarled and swiped at him. Hayden backed away. He wasn't interested in engaging Clint in a fight, but Clint pursued him, the other shifter joining him.

Hayden had no choice but to fight back. The weak voice of his human mind worried over where Shana was. He'd lost sight of her once Clint started attacking. Hayden sustained several deep scratches, but he avoided getting pinned despite the fact he was outnumbered.

In the blur of claws and fur, he heard a roar. Shana leapt upon Clint's back, sinking her teeth into his neck. She threw him under her, pinning him as she held onto his throat, her grip relentless. She gave Hayden time to knock back the other shifter. Deep in the struggle of holding them, Hayden didn't hear the police approaching. He heard the whistle of darts through the air before they landed. He backed off instantly, fearful Shana would get darted. He knew Glen could recognize him in lion form, but he didn't think the officers would be able to quickly ascertain Shana was safe. He dashed toward her. She'd released Clint, but stood above him.

Hayden flinched when the tiny dart sank into her skin. She wobbled and collapsed to the ground. He had to call on every ounce of his humanity to keep from roaring his displeasure. He knew the officers who'd responded were friendly to shifters and a few of them were shifters, but it wouldn't help at all for him to make a scene over what he knew to be an accident. She was an unfamiliar shifter to everyone present other than him. It stood to reason they'd take the safest route and tranquilize her. In the muddle of the following moments, Hayden shifted back into human form.

Glen tossed him some clothes. Shana and the other shifters had shifted back into human form once they collapsed. Hayden knelt at her side.

Glen approached him and handed him a blanket. "We didn't know she was friendly. Sorry about this."

Hayden nodded tightly as he carefully wrapped the blanket around Shana and lifted her in his arms. "Yeah. You couldn't have known who she was. She showed up at the office today right before..." He paused, gesturing toward the other man.

Glen nodded. "Dwight Weber. He's a mid-level dealer. From what we can piece together, he got riled up after we arrested three of his guys. Clint might think he covered his tracks pretty well, but from our interviews today so far, people have been getting pretty damn pissed with how hard he tries to stay away from the dirty work. Too much reward with not enough risk." Glen paused and glanced to Shana. "How about I give you a ride back to your office? If you want, we can stop by Warner's place to get her checked out."

Warner was one of the few doctors in the area who happened to be a shifter. Attempting to explain why Shana had been darted with an animal tranquilizer to any other doctor would be confusing and raise unwanted suspicion.

"That'd be great." Hayden adjusted Shana in his arms and followed Glen to his car.

15

Shana came awake slowly. She rolled her head to the side to find herself looking out a window. The sun was setting over the mountains, its rays casting a soft light through the room. She turned the other way to find she was resting on a couch with a soft, silky blanket tucked around her. Her brain felt fuzzy. She stretched and tried to recall how she got here. She knew she must be at Hayden's house because where else could she be? The last thing she remembered was running through the trees and the skirmish that followed. She remembered the taste of iron in her mouth when she bit into the shifter's neck, but her memory stopped there. She pushed the blanket down and sat up. Her body ached, but she felt okay.

She stretched and stood. Glancing down, she discovered she must have been wearing one of Hayden's shirts. It swallowed her, hanging to her knees, the flannel soft against her skin. She rolled the sleeves up and took in the room. It was a sparsely furnished living room with a couch and two chairs. Though basic, the furniture had luxurious pillows in a soft sage green. Scenic black and white photographs hung on the walls. She heard the sound of water running and followed it, finding Hayden in the kitchen. He stood at the sink rinsing dishes.

"Hey."

He swung around when she spoke. "Shana! You should be resting." He wiped his hands on a dishtowel and tossed it on the counter behind him as he walked in her direction.

When he reached her, he slid his palms down her arms, his touch warm and strong. She brushed her tangled hair out of her eyes. He tried to turn her back in the direction of the living room, but she held firm where she stood. "I'm fine. I don't need to rest. I'm a little tired, but that's it. How did I get here?"

His eyes sobered, and he angled his face down to capture her lips in a kiss. It was brief, but his kiss sent Shana's pulse leaping and desire pooling in her belly. He pulled away, curling his hand around hers and tugging her to the kitchen table.

A while later, Hayden stood to start some coffee. Shana leaned back in her chair. Hayden had given her a quick summary of events for the remainder of the afternoon. "Well, I guess I always knew getting darted with a tranquilizer was a distant possibility."

He turned back to her, shaking his head. "Glen said to send his apologies. They had no way of knowing who you were. The doctor said you'd sleep it off. You feeling okay?"

She nodded. "Pretty much. A little tired, but it's not too bad. Now that Clint's been arrested, along with so many others, what do you think will happen now?"

Hayden leaned against the counter, his eyes warm on hers. "Hard to say. They'll be interviewing for days with the number of people they arrested. According to Glen, the info they had on Clint would put a dent in the local network." He paused to pour two cups of coffee, walking over to the table and handing her one before sitting down across from her. "As far as I'm concerned, I may or may not be around much longer to find out what happens next. With Clint finally held accountable for his part, I feel like I've seen this through as far as I need to."

She took a sip of coffee, savoring the rich flavor. She considered that she'd planned to show up this morning and declare her love, hoping against hope that his feelings held strong for her. On the long flight out here, she'd clung to the memory of his words though doubts filtered in, lingering from the emotional emptiness she'd felt with Callen —the feeling that she wasn't enough, couldn't be enough for any man. She looked across the table to find Hayden's warm caramel gaze on her. In the moment that followed, the air around them heated. Longing rushed through her. She took a breath and forced herself to focus, to remember she had to honor what he'd said to her before he left Catamount.

"You said you'd wait until I was ready."

He nodded slowly. "I meant it." His words were gruff.

Her heart was full, fluttery joy rising inside. "I'm ready."

Hayden's eyes darkened. He hooked his foot on the leg of the chair where she sat and dragged it closer to him. Her skin flushed, heat suffusing her. Her breath became shallow, her low belly clenched and pure fire slid through her veins. She faced him as his palms came to rest on her thighs, his touch a brand. The calloused surface of his skin sent shivers rushing through her as he slowly pushed her thighs apart, his hands curling around her hips and dragging her into his lap. She straddled him, her hair falling around his face. His hands kept moving, coasting up her sides, brushing the curves of her breasts, stroking up her neck and lacing into her hair.

A frisson of awareness traveled up her spine, radiating outward. By the time he brought his mouth to hers, she was shuddering, tossed on the winds of emotion and desire. He was gentle for a brief moment before she twisted herself closer, sweet electricity sizzling between them. Their kiss went wild—hot, wet, and deep—his mouth devouring hers. One of his hands fisted in her hair, tugging her head back, his stubble scraping on the soft skin of her neck as his lips and teeth nibbled their way down. She shoved at his shirt. With one hand, he reached behind his head and yanked it off. He didn't bother with the buttons on the shirt of his she wore, tearing the shirt apart and pushing it off her shoulders.

She was bare underneath save for a pair of black silk panties. The feel of his cock, hard and hot, through the rough denim of his jeans was unbearably arousing. She curled her legs around his hips, riding him, pleasure streaking through her with each shift of her hips. She was soaked in want for him. Her breath came in ragged gasps.

"Shana."

The rough, raw edge to his voice shivered over her skin. She dragged her eyes open to find his waiting—hot and dark. Inside she was pulsing with hot, liquid need. His palm stroked up her back. Heat twisted inside, her core drew tight. She couldn't get close enough to the hard planes of his body, every inch of him pure, lean muscle. Pleasure tightened each time he arched his hips into hers, nudging against her core.

She needed him inside of her. Now. She forced herself to push back and tore his jeans open, shoving them out of the way and freeing his arousal. She curled a hand around it, stroking up and down swiftly before rising. His hand curled on her hip and held her in place, his grip implacable. He stroked a finger across the wet silk. Her breath caught and a whimper escaped her throat. Oh god. She just needed to feel him inside her, to be as close as possible. He pushed the silk out of the way and delved into her wet folds.

"Hayden..."

His name came out on a broken moan. His gaze burned into her. He nudged his cock into her folds, holding still—need sharpened its claws in that hot moment. In a swift surge, he drove into her. She arched back and sank onto him. His hand guiding her, she began to ride him, rolling up and down along his length, the clench of her channel pulsing. Pressure swirled in a storm inside, spinning her tight.

He stayed with her, his body rigid as he rose to meet her hips. Sensation was all she knew and she rode the tide of it until her climax burst through her. He was right behind her. Her channel throbbed around him when he cried out her name, his head slamming back and then forward with the heave of his breath. Pleasure pinged through every cell in her body as the storm of sensation eased. Her head fell into the crook of his shoulder. His hand roughly stroked through her hair.

A while later, they'd untangled themselves, showered and enjoyed a dinner of takeout pizza. Shana stood in the kitchen in yet another of Hayden's shirts. She sipped on a glass of wine. He closed the dishwasher and turned to face her. She stepped close and tipped her head into his chest.

"So, we didn't really talk," she said, her words muffled.

He chuckled, his arms coming around her. Being held close by him felt so good, tears clogged her throat.

"No, no we didn't. I said everything I needed to say the day I left Catamount. Was there something you wanted to say?"

She nodded and lifted her head. "I love you. I'm sorry I got so... I don't know, confused about it. I just needed a little time to sort things out."

His eyes held her, his gaze steady and sure. "As soon as I knew how I felt, you should have been the first to know. I didn't want to pressure you."

"That's the thing. You didn't pressure me. I just..."

He shook his head. "You don't have to explain anything to me. I'm just glad you didn't make me wait longer." He angled his head down, his lips taking hers in a swift kiss. "Love you."

"Love you..." she whispered against his lips. She rested her head on his chest, savoring the sound of his heartbeat.

16

Hayden took a last look around his office. It had been over a month since Clint was arrested. Hayden had been offered Clint's job, but he'd persuaded the department to agree to a transfer to Maine. He would be assuming the regional director position in Maine in a town adjacent to Catamount. The smuggling network wasn't dead in Bozeman, but it had taken a significant hit. Much as Hayden would have liked to think it was gone altogether, he figured it was well on its way. Glen promised to keep him posted if they had any significant developments going forward. Clint was being stubborn so far, refusing to cooperate. Hayden figured Clint was struggling to accept the loss of his power—power in both of his lives.

He flicked the lights off and walked out, carrying a small box containing his personal items. This chapter of his life was closing. Anticipation thrummed through him as he drove away. Shana had returned to Catamount three weeks ago. She needed to get back for work. He spent the remainder of his time here getting organized to move. Even though he'd lived here for years, his life was fairly easy to tidy up. He'd never put roots down. He quickly found a renter to take over the lease on his house. Once he confirmed his work situation, he stayed only until his replacement was hired.

A sense of longing drove him. He missed Shana when she wasn't near and couldn't wait to be by her side again. He waited impatiently for his flight once he got to the airport.

SHANA STOOD in the kitchen at the guesthouse. The scent of onions and garlic permeated the room. She'd been cooking like crazy lately. It offered an outlet for her restless energy while she waited for Hayden to return to Catamount. He'd told her last night he thought he should have everything tied up in another week. Though they talked every morning and every night, she missed him so much it hurt.

Her back was to the door as she added broccoli to the pan, stirring in a mix of brown sugar and soy sauce with ginger. As she reached for the spatula, she heard the door open. Assuming it was Dane or Chloe, she called out a hello.

When there was no response, she glanced over her shoulder to find Hayden striding through the room, a bag slung over his shoulder. Joy soared through her. She whirled around and raced to him. He dropped his bag and caught her in his arms, swinging her around. She peppered his face with kisses. When she pulled back, a tear tipped over her lashes. He wiped it away with his thumb, his own eyes shining with emotion.

"Did I actually pull this off and surprise you?" he asked with a chuckle.

She nodded. "You had me convinced you wouldn't be here any sooner than next week!"

His smile reached into her heart and grabbed hold. He brushed her hair away from her face, tucking a loose lock behind her ear. Shivers chased in the wake of his touch. "Got here as soon as I could," he said gruffly. He fit his mouth over hers in a scorching kiss before pulling away, his breath heaving. "So good to see you."

Warmth unfurled through her. She smiled through her blurry gaze. "You too."

SHANA WALKED across the town green toward Roxanne's Country Store. The air was scented with growth—spring had finally taken hold in Catamount. The bare branches of the trees arching above the green were slowly filling with leaves, green grass had taken hold and flowers abounded. The always early daffodils were a cheery yellow as she walked past a bed of them along the edge of the green. Roxanne had flower boxes adorning every window of the store, so it was a veritable burst of color. Shana pushed through the door and headed straight for the deli in back.

The tables were partially filled as it was

mid-morning. If there was a lull for the store, it was now. Roxanne's back was to the counter while she turned loaves of bread in the brick oven. Shana tapped on the little bell on the counter, purely to annoy Roxanne. Roxanne glanced over her shoulder and rolled her eyes the moment she saw Shana.

"You know that's for when I'm out back, right? When I'm standing two feet away, you can say my name," she offered with a chuckle.

Shana shrugged. "I know. Sometimes I can't help myself."

Roxanne closed the oven and turned around. "Your temporary pass is running out soon."

"My temporary pass?"

"The pass you get for annoying me. It's so good to see you happy again that you get a pass for a little while. After that, I'll throw the oven mitt at you."

Shana grinned. "Right. Can I get a coffee?"

"Of course! Regular or espresso?"

Shana considered for a moment. "Espresso. I have to head into the hospital for an evening shift in a little while."

Roxanne quickly prepped an espresso for her and handed it over. She lingered by the counter after she paid since there weren't any other customers waiting. After a few minutes of casual conversation, Roxanne's eyes turned assessing.

"How are things with Hayden?"

Shana couldn't help the flush that washed through her, not because she was embarrassed, but because the thought of Hayden sent heat flooding through her.

"Good, really good."

Roxanne smiled softly. "You deserve a little slice of happiness. He stops by here almost every morning on his way to work, you know?"

"He loves your coffee and says he's hooked on your ham and cheese savories."

"That's nice, but he's been by enough now I'm not just guessing when I say he's a good guy," Roxanne offered.

Shana chewed her lip. "I know. I still haven't completely adjusted to the fact that he's here and he's with me."

"I figured. Get used to it because that man's ridiculous about you."

Shana's flush deepened. "He is?"

Roxanne rolled her eyes. "As if you need

me to tell you. Yes, seriously." Her eyes sobered. "The past year's been plain shitty for you. Especially when you tack it onto the last few years with Callen. You deserve someone like Hayden." She paused, her eyes moving past Shana.

Shana followed her gaze to see Hayden walking through the grocery aisles toward her. Her breath caught in her throat. He was so damn handsome with his caramel eyes and lean, hard body. As he got closer, she could feel the heat of his gaze from across the room. He strode up to her, smoothly slid a hand into her hair and kissed her. The kiss was brief, but sent liquid heat to her core and flutters twirling in her belly. One stroke of his tongue and he pulled away, nipping her bottom lip as he did.

"Hey," he said, his voice low and just for her.

"Hey." Her pulse pounded, and she scrambled to pull herself together, seeing as they were in a rather public location.

Roxanne cleared her throat. Shana tore her eyes from Hayden's and glanced to Roxanne.

"Don't push it any further, you two. This is a family friendly place," Roxanne said with a shake of her head. She caught Hayden's eyes. "Aren't you usually at work about now?"

Hayden nodded, angling his body away from Shana's and sliding his hand around her hips, his fingers idly stroking the skin just under the edge of her t-shirt. "I'm working now. I'm going to take a look at a new salmon hatchery nearby." His mouth hitched in a wry grin. "I prefer this kind of work over chasing smugglers off protected lands."

"I bet you do," Roxanne countered. "What'll it be for you then?"

"Just coffee. I don't have time to eat, but a pick me up will be perfect."

Roxanne quickly served him. A few other customers arrived, so Shana walked outside with Hayden. His truck was parked right behind her car on the far side of the green. His hand stayed hooked around her waist, his thumb driving her nearly mad with soft strokes just above the waistband of her jeans. When they reached his truck, he set his coffee on the roof and leaned against the truck, tugging her into the cradle of his arms.

"What time will you be home tonight?" he asked, his warm gaze sending hot shivers through her. A blue jay darted behind him, landing beside his coffee and eying it curiously.

"Around eight."

She loved the simple fact that she no longer returned home to an empty house, but rather to the warm, sexy presence of Hayden. They were staying in the guesthouse on Dane and Chloe's property for now, but Hayden had already started making noises about finding a home of their own. While she knew Dane would probably deed the guesthouse to her if she asked, she liked the idea of starting anew in a place of their own.

Hayden nodded. "In that case, I'll take Noah up on his offer to go fishing."

The blue jay got bold and nudged Hayden's coffee cup with its beak. Shana lifted her chin in its direction. "Might want to grab your coffee."

Hayden turned and snatched it away. The blue jay merely lifted itself and resettled further away. Hayden's eyes met hers again. "Gotta go." He leaned forward and took her lips in another breath-stealing, pulse-pounding kiss. When he pulled away, his forehead fell to hers. "I'd rather stay with you all day."

Emotion welled inside, her throat tightening. To be wanted so was something she'd never take for granted. She reached up and brushed a loose lock of hair away from his forehead. "Me too."

EPILOGUE

The following spring, Shana returned home early one evening. The sun was setting, leaving rose and lavender streaks in its wake. She walked along the stone path leading up to the home she shared with Hayden. A few months ago, they'd finally decided on this house and bought it. Close to her childhood home, it was an old stone farmhouse, whose previous owners had completely renovated it. The house boasted a new furnace, appliances, insulation and roof, although it retained its unique charm on the outside.

She pushed through the door, a soft sense of happiness settling over her as she looked around. The entire downstairs was open and airy, light spilling through the tall windows. She set her purse down and put away the groceries before following the sound of voices to the deck out back. When she walked outside, she found Hayden and Dane working on the greenhouse while Chloe sat on the deck, her new baby, Dane Junior, napping beside her in his car seat.

Chloe turned her way with a smile. "Hey there! Hayden thought you'd be home soon. They've been on a mission to finish building the greenhouse today."

Shana looked to the corner of the yard to see her requested greenhouse almost complete. Hayden had drawn up the plans a few weeks ago and done most of the work himself. He'd persuaded Dane to help him with the roof this week. Shana walked to the chair by Chloe and sat down carefully.

Chloe grinned. "I bet you're about ready to have that baby!"

Shana chuckled. "You can say that again. I had no idea I'd reach a point where I wanted to kick this little girl out! I feel like a beached whale whenever I lay down and walking is more of a project than I ever imagined."

Chloe nodded vehemently. "I know. All those baby books gloss over the last few weeks. How soon are you due?"

"Three more weeks, which seems like forever."

Hayden and Dane approached from the yard. Hayden was shirtless, his muscled chest flexing with each swing of his arms. He walked onto the deck and leaned over, bringing his lips right to hers. No matter how many times he kissed her, he took her breath away every time. Even tired, cranky and uncomfortable, heat unfurled inside and her belly fluttered. He slid a hand over her very round belly as he pulled away.

"How're you feeling today?" he asked softly.

"Enormous."

His mouth hitched up at one corner. "You look beautiful."

Tears pricked at her eyes. Before Hayden walked into her life, she'd convinced herself she'd be content simply to escape the barren confines of her previous marriage. Every so often, she paused in wonderment at what she had instead.

She finally managed to tear her eyes away from Hayden's when little Dane let out a cry. Moments later, Dane and Chloe were headed home with little Dane. Shana glanced around their backyard. The house was situated in the foothills of the Appalachian Mountains. An apple orchard was just beyond the grassy lawn and then the forest began further back. The house had passed down through several different families though all had kept the original property intact. They had over fifty acres of their own with wilderness to roam beyond that.

They'd married the month before they bought the house. Shana hadn't wanted a big ceremony. She'd had that with her wedding to Callen, and it had felt as if it were all for show and nothing else. The simple ceremony they had at the local courthouse with friends and family only was perfect.

The sun fell further down the sky, its low rays haloing the trees in the forest. Hayden held his hand out. She placed hers in it and allowed him to tug her slowly to her feet. She'd discovered Hayden was pretty handy in the kitchen. He chalked it up to having lived on his own for so long. He quickly got to work making dinner while she rested on the couch.

Hours later, she woke when Hayden lifted her in his arms. "Did I fall asleep on the couch again?"

His laughter rumbled against her ear where her head rested on his shoulder. "Yup."

"You know, I can walk myself to bed."

He paused in the doorway, nudging the light switch with his elbow. When she looked up, his gaze seared into her. "I know. Just like I can carry you to bed."

At that, his lips caught hers.

Thank you for reading Destined Mate - I hope you loved Shana & Hayden's story!

For more steamy, small town shifter romance, Roxanne & Max's story is next in A Catamount Christmas. Fiery Roxanne had her heart broken by Max and now he's back in Catamount. He's just as sexy and smoldering as ever...and he wants a second chance. Don't miss Max's story!

Keep reading for a sneak peek!

Be sure to sign up for my newsletter for the latest news, teasers & more! Click here to sign up: http://jhcroixauthor.com/subscribe/

EXCERPT: A CATAMOUNT CHRISTMAS

Roxanne Morgan spun around and passed a sandwich over the counter, immediately turning to take the order of the next person in line. She was covering the deli counter for lunch at the small business she owned—a grocery store, hardware store and deli all rolled into one.

"What'll it be?" she asked, her eyes quickly scanning the area beyond the counter. When there was no reply, she glanced up. Her heart stuttered and then lunged forward into a wild pounding.

"Hey Roxy," the man standing across the counter said.

Roxanne didn't find herself speechless very often, but at the moment, she couldn't seem to form a word. Max Stone stood in front of her—the one and only boy she'd ever loved, the boy who'd broken her heart when he left Catamount, Maine...and their love behind. Her eyes soaked him in—his mahogany brown hair, his amber eyes, and his lanky, muscled body. He wore a black down jacket, unzipped to reveal a charcoal gray shirt and faded jeans. His gaze coasted over her. She felt bare and exposed, and frantically tried to gather herself together inside.

Her cheeks felt hot, but she ignored it. She could do this. All she had to do was be polite. Her body was only reacting because she hadn't seen Max in so long. It was an echo of their past and nothing more. "Hey Max. Haven't seen you around in years," she finally replied, her words belying the turmoil she felt inside.

The truth was it had been precisely fifteen years since Max had been in Catamount. He had moved away with his mother after his father died in an accident at the mill in a nearby town. Roxanne and Max had started dating the year before, and she'd loved him in the way only youth allowed—head over heels infatuation mingled with the rosy yearning to be together forever. The hopes of youth had kept her tendency toward cynicism at bay, and she'd flung herself into their relationship. One afternoon when Max was supposed to come over, he'd called instead. In a conversation that lasted maybe five minutes, he told her his father had died, they were moving, and he broke up with her. She'd been too stunned to fully absorb what he said. A few days later when she managed to cobble together a coherent thought, she'd raced over to his house to try to talk to him and found his family's home locked up. No one answered the door after she knocked for what felt like hours.

She'd swung between the emotional poles of grief, about his father and about the abrupt end of their relationship. She'd stuffed her grief away and done her damnedest to move on. The first few years after he left, she would occasionally wonder if she might hear from him, or if he would return to Catamount. She finally gave up hoping and wishing, but she never quite got over Max.

Now, he stood here before her and a tornado of feelings swirled through her—confusion, hope, joy, anger, sadness and more. She twirled a pen between her fingers and wondered what to do. A small part of her wanted to storm past him and not look back, just the way he'd left her all those years ago. She couldn't do that though because she owned Roxanne's Country Store. An arc of annoyance flashed through her. Max was showing up in the heart of her world.

"It's really good to see you, Roxy," Max said, cutting through her short walk down memory lane.

Max happened to be the only person who'd ever called her Roxy with any regularity. It chafed to hear him call her that now.

She willed herself to stay calm. Still struggling to form words sensibly, she nodded. She couldn't quite bring herself to say it was good to see him. She was relieved when another customer stepped to the counter.

Hank Anderson, Catamount's police chief, leaned against the counter. "Hey Roxanne, can I get the usual today?"

Roxanne glanced to Hank. "Sure. Give me a sec." She forced a smile and turned away to pour a cup of coffee for Hank. At the moment, she would have given just about anything to have Becky here to help this morning. Becky was one of her regular deli employees and would normally be here, but she'd called in sick with a nasty cold. Roxanne was reconsidering how relieved she'd been to not be exposed to whatever the hell Becky had. She sounded like she was on the verge of death when she called, so Roxanne had happily supported her staying home until she was better. But now, with Max here, Roxanne didn't have any back up, so she couldn't busy herself in the back of the kitchen. She had no choice but to stay here and somehow fumble through the next few minutes. She prayed Max wouldn't stay long. As she fitted the lid over Hank's coffee, she heard him start talking to Max and anxiety tightened in her chest.

"Max Stone? Damn, haven't seen you around in years! How are ya?" Hank asked.

Roxanne turned back to face them, gripping Hank's coffee tightly in her hand. Max grinned over at Hank. "Hey Hank, it's good to see you. It might have been a long time, but I'm back to stay."

Roxanne felt as if she were falling inside. Max was back to stay? So many questions tumbled through her mind, she couldn't think clearly. She mentally shook herself. It had been fifteen years. She was long past her youthful love for him, and he'd clearly never felt the same way. If he had, she didn't see how he could have left things between them the way he did and then just walk in here casually. Anger rose inside, but she batted it back. She needed to stay calm and not make a scene.

Max and Hank were still talking when she turned and took the few steps to the counter. She set Hank's coffee down and slid it over. "Here you go"

Hank snagged it and took a gulp. "Ahh. Perfect." He pulled his wallet out, glancing between Roxanne and Max as he did. "Did you two stay in touch all these years?" Hank asked.

His question was innocent enough, but it sent another flash of anger through Roxanne. She wasn't up for nosy questions. She busied herself taking the ten-dollar bill Hank handed over and getting his change from the register, her ears perked to see how Max responded to Hank's question.

"Unfortunately not," Max replied. "Things were a little hectic that first year after my dad died, and I wasn't thinking too clearly."

Roxanne couldn't stop herself from looking over to Max. His amber eyes caught hers. "Roxanne was the first person I looked for when I got here, so I'm hoping we'll have time to catch up."

Hank chuckled. "Roxanne's Country Store here is still the heart and soul of Catamount. She's done her family proud running it the way she does." Hank took another swallow of coffee. "Anyway, good to see you, Max. If you need anything, just stop by. Where you staying?"

"My mom never sold our old house, so I'm planning to renovate it. Until then, I booked a room at the inn down the street."

Hank pushed away from the counter. "Well, you've got your work cut out for you. Don't think anybody's been there since you left."

Something flashed in Max's eyes. Once upon a time, Roxanne might have thought it was pain, but she wouldn't know right now. Though her body was spinning with heat and the familiarity of Max's presence, her mind was bolting steel doors around her heart and insisting she not go thinking she knew him the way she once did.

"I'm sure I do. I plan to head up there in a little bit to take a look. Good to see you, Hank."

"If you need any help, let me know. I'm sure I can round up a few kids from the high school to help out with the land clearing. They're young and too strong to worry about their backs yet," Hank said as he lifted his coffee cup in a farewell and turned away.

Max turned back to the counter. For a long moment, he didn't say anything. He simply looked at her, his eyes coasting over her face and dipping down before returning. Her cheeks heated when his gaze met hers again. "I'm guessing this feels kind of out of the blue for you, huh?"

Her heart in her throat, Roxanne nodded.

Max curled his hands on the edge of the counter. "I have enough sense to know now probably isn't a great time to talk, but I just need you to know I'm sorry. I couldn't have stopped my mom from up and leaving Catamount the way we did right after my dad died, but I shouldn't have broken things off with you the way I did."

Another customer approached the counter. Gail Anderson, Hank's wife, stepped to Max's side. "I just saw Hank on his way out," Gail said, not even bothering with a perfunctory greeting.

With her mind spinning over what Max

had just said, Roxanne turned to Gail, barely able to think. She must have managed to nod because Gail huffed. "I told him I was only running a few minutes behind!" Gail's blue eyes snapped. Gail and Hank were long-time Catamount residents, both born and raised here, and entwined in the community. Hank was the police chief and Gail was a retired schoolteacher. Gail glanced to her side, her eyes widening. "Max Stone?"

Oh. My. God. Just how many of these moments am I going to have to survive? Well, Max's family was here for a long time before they left. Anyone that knew him is going to be startled to see him. You'd better get used to this. Roxanne mentally sighed as she tried to marshal her thoughts. *It might mean nothing that Max said he shouldn't have broken things off the way he did. He might not have felt the way you did anyway, he just feels bad about how he handled it. Don't go thinking it's anything other than that. Just act normal and get through this.*

Roxanne cued in to the conversation between Max and Gail. "I decided to move back last summer after my mom died. Her sister was the reason we moved there, and she died the year before, so there was nothing left holding me there. I missed Catamount the entire time we were gone, so I decided it was time to come home," Max said.

Gail looked between Max and Roxanne, her eyes considering. She appeared about to say something, but she stayed quiet for several beats. "Well, it's nice to have you back. I missed your mother. I'm sorry to hear she passed away."

Max nodded solemnly. "I wish she'd had a chance to get back here before she died."

Gail nodded firmly. "It is what it is. Everyone will be glad to know you're here." She turned to Roxanne. "I was supposed to meet Hank for coffee, but since he couldn't be bothered to wait, I'll get some to go."

Roxanne felt like she was in a surreal dream. On autopilot, she swung around and poured a cup of coffee for Gail. Moments later, Gail was walking through the deli and down one of the grocery aisles to the front door.

When Roxanne turned back to Max, she forced herself to keep it light because she couldn't deal with anything else right now. "What can I get for you?" she asked, her words coming out smoothly only because she'd said them thousands of times.

MAX LOOKED over at Roxanne and tamped down the urge to leap over the counter and pull her into his arms. She stood there before him, her blonde hair pulled back in a haphazard ponytail, loose curls escaping and framing her heart-shaped face. Her blue eyes were as gorgeous as he remembered—wide eyes that tipped up at the corners, the blue so rich he could lose himself in it.

Not a day had passed since he left when he didn't think about her, and here she stood before him—taking his breath away. Fifteen years later, she'd filled out and her figure was all curves—generous breasts, an hourglass dip at her waist, and lush hips. She emanated a strength and power she hadn't had back when they were young. She'd always been strong and independent, so it didn't surprise him to sense those qualities had blossomed within her.

Max had so much to say, yet now clearly was not the time or place. Roxanne's Country Store was bustling. The deli area where they were now had customers seated at tables scattered throughout the small area. The rest of the store, a mix of groceries, hardware and just about everything, had customers meandering through the aisles as they filled shopping baskets. This place held so many memories for him, it was almost overwhelming.

AVAILABLE NOW!

A Catamount Christmas

GO HERE to sign up for information on new releases: http://jhcroixauthor.com/subscribe/

FIND MY BOOKS

Thank you for reading Destined Mate! I hope you enjoyed the story. If so, you can help other readers find my books in a variety of ways.

1) Write a review!
2) Sign up for my newsletter, so you can receive information about upcoming new releases & receive a FREE copy of one of my books: http://jhcroixauthor.com/subscribe/
3) Like and follow my Amazon Author page at https://amazon.com/author/jhcroix
4) Follow me on Bookbub at https://www.bookbub.com/authors/j-h-croix
5) Follow me on Instagram at https://www.instagram.com/jhcroix/

6) Like my Facebook page at https://www.
facebook.com/jhcroix

CATAMOUNT LION SHIFTERS
Protected Mate
Chosen Mate
Fated Mate
Destined Mate
A Catamount Christmas
The Lion Within
Lion Lost & Found
Swoon Series
This Crazy Love
Wait For Me
Break My Fall
Truly Madly Mine
Into The Fire Series
Burn For Me
Slow Burn
Burn So Bad
Hot Mess
Burn So Good
Sweet Fire
Play With Fire
Melt With You
Burn For You

Crash & Burn
Brit Boys Sports Romance
The Play
Big Win
Out Of Bounds
Play Me
Naughty Wish
Diamond Creek Alaska Novels
When Love Comes
Follow Love
Love Unbroken
Love Untamed
Tumble Into Love
Christmas Nights
Last Frontier Lodge Novels
Christmas on the Last Frontier
Love at Last
Just This Once
Falling Fast
Stay With Me
When We Fall
Hold Me Close
Crazy For You
Just Us

ACKNOWLEDGMENTS

Massive thanks to my readers for giving me the courage to take the leap into paranormal romance. It's been a blast and your encouragement and enthusiasm means more than words can convey. Laura Kingsley edits my work with a discerning eye and keeps pushing me to make each book better. Clarise Tan at CT Cover Creations weaves designing magic with my covers. Always, my husband - the man who's handy with names when I need them and graciously gives me the time and space to write like crazy.

. . .

xoxo
J.H. Croix

ABOUT THE AUTHOR

USA Today Bestselling Author J. H. Croix lives in a small town in the historical farmlands of Maine with her husband and two spoiled dogs. Croix writes contemporary romance with sassy women and alpha men who aren't afraid to show some emotion. Her love for quirky small-towns and the characters that inhabit them shines through in her writing. Take a walk on the wild side of romance with her bestselling novels!

Places you can find me:
jhcroixauthor.com
jhcroix@jhcroix.com

www.ingramcontent.com/pod-product-compliance
Lightning Source LLC
Chambersburg PA
CBHW060806210726
48292CB00013B/1909